SUMMER CAMP CREEPS

Other Avon Camelot Books by
Tim Schoch

CREEPS
FLASH FRY, PRIVATE EYE

TIM SCHOCH grew up in New Jersey and graduated from the University of Tampa with a degree in Drama. He has been a full-time actor and singer and is currently Copy Chief for a major New York City publisher. *Creeps* and *Flash Fry, Private Eye,* his first two Avon Camelot novels for young readers, continue to be successes. He has also written three mysteries for adults, dozens of humorous newspaper and magazine pieces, and more than 250 songs, some of which he has performed in a musical-comedy act with his partner, Jerry Winsett. Tim says he gets many of his story ideas from his son, Derek (though Derek doesn't know it). He lives with his wife, Wendy McCurdy, in New Jersey.

SUMMER CAMP CREEPS

Tim Schoch

AN AVON  CAMELOT BOOK

SUMMER CAMP CREEPS is an original publication of Avon Books. This work has never before appeared in book form.

AVON BOOKS
A division of
The Hearst Corporation
105 Madison Avenue
New York, New York 10016

Library of Congress Cataloging in Publication Data:

Schoch, Tim.
  Summer camp creeps.

  (An Avon Camelot book)
  Summary: Jeffrey and his friend Gwen take turns describing the rivalry between the boys and the girls one strange weekend at Camp Arrowhead, when a mysterious thief strikes repeatedly in the night.
  [1. Camps—Fiction. 2. Mystery and detective stories] I. Title.
PZ7.S36476Su   1987   [Fic]   87-949

First Camelot Printing: July 1987

CAMELOT TRADEMARK REG. U.S. PAT. OFF. AND IN OTHER COUNTRIES, MARCA REGISTRADA, HECHO EN U.S.A.

Printed in the U.S.A.

OPM   10   9   8   7   6   5   4   3   2   1

To Dad,
in the summer
of his new life

I've Gotta Tell You Something

IF you looked at the title of this book you already know that someone went to summer camp. I did. Other kids went, too. But I'm not one of the creeps. I guess you could say I'm the hero. I'm Jeff Moody.

Wild and exciting things happened at Camp Arrowhead. I'll be telling you all about how brave and smart us boys were. You'll really love it.

Gwen Sharp, my know-it-all friend, will be telling you about the girls—even though they weren't too brave or smart. Gwen was camping with the girls, so she knows all about the sneaky and stupid things they did to cheat and get us guys in big trouble.

Gwen thinks she's a hero, too. Har-dee-har-har.

Now Wait Just a Minute

HI. I'm Gwen Sharp. Please, don't believe anything Jeffrey tells you. At first, he didn't even want me to tell the girls' side of the story. He said that nobody wants to read about sissy girls. Well, I said that if it weren't for the girls there wouldn't even *be* a story. He said, "Oh, yeah?" I said, "Yeah!" And since I'm taller than he is, I won. So, thanks to me, you'll get the truth about what *really* happened that strange weekend at Camp Arrowhead.

Just wait until you see all the horrible, juvenile, babyish things the boys did to the girls. That's why we had to get back at them, don't you see? Someone had to teach those boys a lesson.

So, take it from me: Jeff and the boys had nothing at all to har-dee-har-har about.

Jeff

SREEERRRK! The smelly blue bus stopped in a cloud of dust.

"Camp Arrowhead. Everybody out," the skinny woman driver said.

Eleven kids were on the bus. It was 7:45 on a hot Friday morning in July. Most of us were yawning and rubbing gunk out of our eyes.

I was in the front seat with my beat-up black sneakers propped up on the rail. When I looked out the window I saw about a million trees, a huge green lake, and a long wooden building that looked like it had been built back when Abraham Lincoln was president of the United States. A sign on the building said: CAMP ARROWHEAD LODGE.

So this is where I'd be stuck for the weekend. Oh, boy.

"Jeffrey, this place looks great!" said Gwen Sharp, who was sitting up straight beside me. I didn't know how she could see anything with all those fingerprints on her glasses.

"I'm getting itchy already thinking about all the bugs out there," I said.

"Not me," Gwen said. "This place is history, J.M. It's Indian country. Real Indians. Hunting, fishing, living in teepees. Dad says this whole camp is loaded with Indian artifacts. Pottery. Arrowheads. Graves."

"Really?" I took another look out the window and into the forest. Indians. I could almost see them scouting the hilltops, paddling a canoe through the reeds of the lake, flicking arrows at a huge grizzly bear. Suddenly I couldn't wait to get out of the bus.

After we thumped our suitcases down the steps of the bus, a guy with a crew cut and bulging muscles waved a clipboard in the air to quiet us down.

"Welcome to Camp Arrowhead," he said. "This just might be the best weekend of your lives."

"Or the last," said Dave Larson, my nutty freckle-faced friend.

We all laughed.

The guy went on. "My name is Albert Nord. You can call me Al." He pointed a thumb at the beautiful blonde woman next to him. "This is my wife, Ellie. You can call her Ellie. Ha-ha."

Nobody laughed.

"We run this camp," Al said. "Right now, let's see if everyone is here."

He looked down at his clipboard and started calling off names. Most of the kids I knew, but some of them I didn't.

"Mack Buster."

"Here."

"Judy Kamin."

"Here."

"Kenny Kamin."

"Here."

"Kaybee Keeper."

6

"This place."

Al Nord looked up. "What was that?"

"I am here, in this place," Kaybee said, smiling.

The kids giggled. Kaybee was wearing a black T-shirt. On the front in big pink letters were the words: BELIEVE IN THE MARS FACE.

"Dave Larson."

"I'm in *this* place."

We all broke up. Dave's my best buddy.

"Frederick McFink."

"Here."

He's not my best buddy or anybody's best buddy. We call him Crunch because of what he likes to do to us.

"Jeffrey Moody."

"Bingo!" I said. Nobody laughed. Oh, well.

"Patricia Nickle."

"I'm here, but call me Pinky."

"Carmen Piro."

"Here."

"Gwendolyn Sharp."

"Here."

"Tandy Thomas."

Silence.

"Tandy Thomas?"

"She'll be here," Gwen said. "She told me she would."

"Thank you," Al Nord said, going back to his list.

"Vincent Tuttle."

"Here."

Vince was the fattest kid I'd ever seen in my life.

"Well," Al Nord said. "Only Tandy is missing."

Just then a car horn blasted through the woods. We all turned and saw a gleaming silver Cadillac roaring down the dirt road. It came to a halt right in front of the lodge. Tandy's father was driving and her mother sat beside him.

7

Tandy was slouched down in the backseat, hiding behind her frizzy blonde hair. The window was open a little and we could hear what they were saying.

"I don't wanna go!" Tandy whined.

"Oh, you'll just love it, honey," Tandy's mother said. "Look, your friends are all waiting for you. Now be a good girl, go on."

"I don't wanna!" Tandy said.

Tandy's father slapped the steering wheel and said in a low voice. "If you don't get out of this car, you can forget about going to Hawaii next month."

In five seconds, Tandy was out and waving good-bye to her parents. Then Tandy turned and faced us like we were all waiting to throw mud balls at her or something.

"Tandy Thomas?" Al Nord said.

Tandy nodded, wiping tears from her eyes.

"Welcome to Camp Arrowhead."

Tandy just stared at him.

"Okay, everybody," Al Nord announced, "inside the lodge for a powwow."

"A powwow?" I said to Dave.

Dave smiled. "Isn't that the way an Indian dog barks?"

I broke up.

Behind me, Gwen was helping Tandy with her luggage.

"Neat place, isn't it?" Gwen said.

"I've never seen a more filthy, disgusting place in my whole life," said spoiled-rotten Tandy.

Gee, I thought, she sure will be loads of fun.

We followed Al Nord—Dave was already calling him Al Nerd—into a large cafeteria with wooden walls, a wooden ceiling, and long wooden tables and benches that were kind of greasy feeling.

"Everybody have a seat," Ellie Nerd said, tossing back her long blonde hair with a jerk of her head.

8

"I think I'm in love," Dave said, staring at Mrs. Nerd.

"Since when can you think?" Crunch McFink said.

Al Nerd brought two people out of the kitchen: a man and a woman. The man was very short with a big pot belly. The woman was very tall and as skinny as the edge of a door.

"I'd like to introduce Otto Asterman and his wife Happy," Al said, flexing his muscles even when he didn't want to. "They are the cooks. And you'd better be nice to them. If you're not, you might just find a nice, fat dragonfly at the bottom of your soup."

Happy and Otto Asterman laughed hard.

Us kids sure didn't. We waved and smiled and tried to be as nice as we could.

"Now," Al Nerd said, "as Otto and Happy pass out some juice and cookies, I'll be passing out the camp schedule for the weekend."

Each of us got two chocolate chip cookies and a tall glass of red juice that Dave immediately called "dragonfly blood." After we got the camp schedules, Al Nerd started talking again.

"Don't lose these schedules, and don't be late for any of the events. You have a lot to look forward to."

Then we all got to pick who we would share a tent with. Dave and I picked each other. Crunch chose quiet Mack Buster. Judy Kamin and Carmen Piro got together, and so did Kenny Kamin and fat Vince Tuttle. Gwen and Kaybee decided to share a tent, but sulking Tandy wasn't choosing anybody.

"Look," Pinky Nickle said to Tandy, "it looks like I'm stuck with you. You can be in my tent if you don't whine all the time." In school, snotty Pinky tried her best to make all the other girls worship her. And Tandy wanted nothing more than to have Pinky like her.

9

"You want me to share a tent with you?" Tandy said. "Sure, Pinky, sounds great. We'll have loads of fun."

Pinky rolled her eyes. "Calm down. Just do as I say and we'll get along fine."

"Okay, all settled?" Al Nerd said. "Now, come up here and tell me who you are sharing a tent with. Then, go out to your assigned tents, drop off your things, and get ready for the big, exciting volleyball game!"

Yippee.

"This was a great idea—coming to this camp," Gwen said to me. "We're going to have a blast."

"Yeah," I said. "I can't wait to go exploring and canoeing."

"Let's do some stuff together, okay, Jeffrey?"

"Sure! See you later."

I was glad my good buddy Gwen was there.

Soon, we were all moving into our tents, which were across the road from the lodge and up at the edge of the woods. The boys' tents were grouped to the right, the girls' tents to the left. The counselors got to live in the lodge. In the back of each group of tents was a low wooden building—the toilets and showers.

The tents were pretty big and smelled like moldy socks. Inside were two narrow metal beds and two small dressers. As Dave unpacked, I flicked a black bug off my bed and stretched out. I could feel the mattress buttons sticking me in the back.

"So what do you think about the schedule?" I asked Dave.

"Looks pretty neat," he said. "The volleyball game sounds boring. We'll kill the girls."

"Naturally," I said.

"This place is great, Jeff. All sorts of Indian things are all over the place."

10

"And no parents to tell us what to do," I said.

"Yeah. We can do whatever we want!" Dave said.

"So, what do you want to do now?"

Dave shrugged. "Beats me. Maybe I'll count my freckles. Got a mirror?"

I laughed. Dave is a riot.

Suddenly Crunch started screaming from the next tent over. "I said, that's my side! And leave the tent flap closed!"

Dave and I rushed out of our tent and went next door. Flabby Vince Tuttle came rolling over, too. We peeked inside and saw Crunch ball up the front of Mack's shirt.

"Hey, Crunch," I said, "I thought we're supposed to be having fun here."

"Maybe you creeps can have fun with this sissy stuff, but not me."

"So why don't you just go home?" Dave said.

"And chicken out?" Crunch said. "I never chicken out. I'm staying, and that's that. So, beat it."

"Oh, come on now," Vince said, smiling wide with his wide face. "We all know you're tough, but let's stick together, okay?"

"My fist'll stick to your face if you don't beat it," Crunch said.

Dave, Vince, and I left. When we turned around, Gwen was standing there with all the girls around her.

"Hi!" she said, all peppy-like. "Ready for the big volleyball game?"

"You bet," Dave said.

Blubbery Vince roared, "This boy is ready, you can bet on that. Let's volley some balls!"

We all ran off to the volleyball court, which was way down past our tents. Soon, Al and Ellie Nerd arrived with a volleyball.

11

"Right on time," Al Nerd said. "I can see you're going to be the best group we've ever had."

Boy, is this guy a jerk, I thought.

"Okay. It's the boys against the girls. Boys on one side of the net, girls on the other side. To make the scoring quicker, we play by Camp Arrowhead rules. That means, if you miss a shot, the other team gets a point, no matter which team serves. Each team gets five serves. Get it? Good. We play to twenty-one. Go on, practice a little."

We practiced a little.

"We'll kill 'em, no problem," fat Vince said. "Heck, we could spot the girls five points and we'd still smear 'em!"

"*Ten* points!" Crunch said.

"You've got it," Al Nerd said with a grin. "The boys kindly give the girls ten points to start."

Vince's and Crunch's smiles vanished. All the girls giggled.

Soon, with the girls already winning ten to zero, Al Nerd blew his stupid whistle and the volleyball game began.

Pinky served the ball over the net. It hit Kenny's legs and bounced away. The girls cheered.

Eleven to zero.

Pinky served again. KA-BLOOM! Big Vince mashed it right back for a point.

"Take that!" Vince bellowed, laughing.

"Good going, Turtle," Crunch said.

Eleven to one.

"Come one, girls," Gwen said. "We can beat these guys."

Pinky served again. This time Mack butted it with his head. The ball flew up and landed right on top of Kaybee's head.

"Get with it Kaybee!" Pinky screamed at her.

"She's just warming up," Gwen said.

"Yes," Kaybee said, "I'm just starting my fire."

Eleven to two.

Pinky served again. The ball came to me. I tapped it over to Dave who tapped it back to Mack who tapped it to Crunch who KA-BLOOM! smashed it over the net and smack onto Carmen's foot. She started hopping around and us guys broke up.

"Eleven to three," Vince said. "Girls, you don't have a chance. Right, Kenny?"

Shy Kenny Kamin just stood there with his hands at his sides. He was short enough to look under the net to his older sister, Judy, who might as well have been a statue of an unhappy girl.

"The game's not over yet," Gwen said. "Let's go, girls!"

Pinky served for the last time. But it was too low. It hit the top edge of the net and thwanged back and bopped Tandy right in the forehead.

"Ow!" Tandy screamed.

"Eleven to four!" flabby Vince hollered at the girls.

Now it was Crunch's turn to serve. KA-BLOOM!

Eleven to five.

The game went on.

POW! BANG! BOP!

The girls got better, but we boys won twenty-one to eighteen.

It was a great game, a great game. Victory felt good. Us guys were dancing around, screaming and patting one another on the back. The girls just slumped around, looking sad.

"Hey, Pinky," Crunch hollered, "how's it feel to be a *loser!*"

13

"You shut up!" Pinky snapped.

"Easy," Gwen said. "It's just a friendly game, remember?"

"Sure we're friends," blimp Vince said. "But some of us are winners, and some of us are losers. And, sorry girls, us boys will always be the winners! Yaaay!"

We cheered and danced around some more and rubbed it in to the girls some more, then ran back to our tents like we'd just won the Olympics.

Lunchtime.

We were all yapping as we entered the cafeteria. When Tandy came in, I noticed a round red mark on her forehead where the volleyball had smacked her. Ooo, that must have hurt. I felt kind of sorry for her.

"You okay?" I asked her.

"No, I'm not okay," she snapped. "I've got a headache, my new sneakers are dirty, and I'm actually sweaty. I'm totally grossed out, so leave me alone."

"Fine," I said. "One less girl to worry about as we beat you at sports."

"Be nice, J.M.," Gwen said.

"Zipping zeppers!" It was strange Kaybee Keeper with her wild reddish hair and pink and yellow jeans. Kaybee was a stargazer, into astronomy. Even her ceiling at home was painted like a huge map of the nighttime sky. She had started talking strangely just to be different, and she never broke the habit. In fact, I kind of liked the way she talked. "You care more about thumping sports than about Tandy's sad face?"

"Maybe," I said, scratching my head.

"Come on, Gwendolyn," Kaybee said. "I thought Jeffrey was a heartsome person, but he's beginning to change my mind."

Gwen, Kaybee, and Tandy walked off to get some food.

14

"Talking to the losers?" fat Vince said to me.

"Yeah," Crunch said, "don't get too close to them, Jeff. Losing might rub off. Ha!"

"Shut up!" Pinky yelled. The rest of the girls didn't like Crunch's remark either.

I went up and got a hamburger, fries, and container of milk, then sat down with the guys.

The girls sat at their own table, whispering to one another and glaring at us. We sat two tables away, smirking at them. They didn't like losing, and they sure didn't like us rubbing it in.

Then it happened.

"Hey!" Crunch yelled. He stood and pointed a finger across the room at Carmen. "Who are you sticking your tongue out at?"

Carmen stood up. "You!"

Fat Vince slowly rose. "You can't talk to my buddy like that!"

Pinky stood. "Oh, yeah? Who's gonna make her stop?"

Dave stood. "A truck already made her stop! It stopped right on her face!"

All the girls stood up.

"You think you're so great just because you won a dumb volleyball game?" Gwen said.

All the boys stood up.

"Yeah, we do," Crunch hollered. "And we're going to kill you at everything!"

"Never!" Pinky shouted. "Us girls are tougher than you wimps!"

"Prove it!" Vince shouted. "Anytime you say!"

Pinky screamed at the top of her lungs: "How about *NOW!*"

Pinky sent half a hamburger spinning across the room. It smacked, ketchup side down, on Vince's huge belly.

15

Steam almost came out of Vince's ears. He took a long, deep breath and roared: "FOOOOOOOD FIIIIGHT!"

The next thing I knew I got hit in the face with a pickle. The air came alive with zooming food. Milk, dragonfly blood, french fries, you name it. Everything was flying around like gravity suddenly took the day off.

"Stop! Stop! Stop!" Al Nerd stood between our tables with his hands in the air. "Stop it right now, or you all go home!"

One by one, we sat down.

Al Nerd looked over at his wife, Ellie. She was trying really hard to hide her giggles.

"In all my seven years of running this camp," Al Nerd said, "this is the very first food fight we ever had. Girls, I want you to stop antagonizing the boys."

"What!" Gwen said.

Al Nerd held up a finger. "I know who started this fight. I saw Pinky throw that hamburger."

"But they were picking on us!" Pinky said.

Al Nerd shook his head. "Look, don't be such sore losers. Pinky, I want you to apologize to the boys."

"Never," she said.

"If you want to remain at this camp, Pinky, you'll apologize. We don't tolerate troublemakers here."

Pinky was about to explode. The other boys and I just sat there with huge toothy grins plastered on our faces.

"Sorry," Pinky said quickly, frowning hard. All the girls gave us mean glares.

Then we heard a sound. It was Kenny Kamin. He was hunched under the table crying into his knees. His sister, Judy, ran over and helped him out. She put her arm around his shoulders and brought him up to Al Nerd.

"We want to go home now," she said. "We don't like your camp."

16

So Kenny and Judy went off to call their parents. The rest of us had to clean up the mess we'd made in the cafeteria.

I tried to say something to Gwen, but she ignored me, probably because I accidentally flapped her in the face with a french fry.

Soon the girls, all in one group, left.

"Gee," fat Vince said, "I never finished my hamburger."

"There's one over there in the corner," Dave said.

Mack laughed hard at that.

"Guys," I said, "we've got nothing to worry about. We can handle anything the girls dish out."

"Right!" Vince said.

"Speak for yourself," Crunch said. "I'm sick of these stupid games already."

"Would you rather play with the girls?" I said.

"Would you like me to rip your face off?" Crunch said to me.

I wouldn't.

Hippo Vince patted Crunch on the back. "You can't fool this boy, Crunch. I saw you having fun out there on the court. You and me, we're going to be heroes when this is over, you'll see."

Crunch tried to hold back a smile. "You really are a turtle, Tuttle, you know that?"

"Whether we like it or not," I said, "we're stuck with each other. Let's have some fun, huh?"

"Fun? With five girl enemies out there?" Dave said. "I'll tell you guys, unless I'm wrong, we're in for some really *un*-funny trouble."

Dave wasn't wrong.

Gwen

IT was just not fair. Perhaps Pinky shouldn't have thrown that hamburger, but the boys *had* been picking on us ever since they won that volleyball game. And Al Nord blamed *us*. I was furious and determined to get even with the boys. We just *had* to win the next game. Unfortunately, Pinky had different ideas of how to fight back.

"We cheat. We steal. We sneak in the night and strike during the day," Pinky was saying.

"Is that honest?" Kaybee asked.

"Of course not," Pinky replied. "But after what they did to us, they deserve it."

"Can't we just forget about it?" Tandy asked hesitantly.

"Be quiet, you wimp," Pinky snapped at her.

We were all standing out in the sunshine in front of the lodge. Looking through the front and back windows to the lake, we could see the boys shuffling around the shoreline and skipping stones across the water.

"Revenge is the only answer," Pinky said. "Anybody have any ideas how we can get back at those jerks?"

I was shocked. Almost everybody had some sort of tricky idea.

While they talked, I went up to my tent to change my ketchup-splattered T-shirt. While switching shirts, I noticed on the schedule that after our hike around the lake, which was next, I'd have some free time. The perfect chance to read some more of *Gone with the Wind*. I opened my suitcase to get the paperback—but it wasn't there. Then I remembered I'd stuck it under my pillow. It wasn't there either. I clawed through everything I owned. My book was gone!

I ran down to the lodge and found Al Nord out back talking with the boys. The girls followed me.

"Somebody stole my copy of *Gone with the Wind!*"

"Are you sure?" he asked.

"I'm certain," I said. "It was right in my suitcase, and now it's gone!"

"Yeah, it's gone with the wind!" Dave said.

Al Nord laughed.

"I don't think it's so funny," I said. "And I think one of the boys took it to get back at us for the food fight."

Al Nord continued smiling. "Well, if they did, it's not the end of the world. Little practical jokes like this always go on at camp. I'm sure your book will turn up, Gwen."

Pinky pulled me aside. "Forget it, Gwen. Nord's sticking up for the guys again. You can't win."

"I think you're right," I said. I was really burned up.

All the kids started chattering, wondering who stole my book and blaming one another.

Al Nord seemed to have forgotten about it immediately. He was waving his hands, attempting to introduce us to the person who would be leading us on the hike around Lake Hoppipong.

"Kids, meet John Redwing," Al Nord said. "Redwing

is part Indian. His ancestors lived and hunted on this land. In fact, John himself lives all summer on the other side of the lake in a teepee like his forefathers. If you listen, you can learn a lot from him.''

John Redwing didn't look much older than we were, maybe fifteen. He was stringy and strong, with very short dark hair and the scariest black eyes I'd ever seen.

"Everything has a story," Redwing said. "This whole campgrounds is a story, a history of a noble people who were here long before your ancestors even dreamed of coming across the ocean. In this ground are the bones of my people. Their life is here, too. You will learn and see some of it. Come with me, children, and witness where American life began.'' He took off, walking with huge strides.

"He's weird," Dave whispered to Jeffrey.

"Don't make fun of him," Crunch said to Dave, "or he'll scalp you.''

"That's an ignorant remark," I snapped. "Most Indians weren't violent at all, especially the tribes around here.''

"Miss Encyclopedia strikes again," Vince said.

"I know I'm going to get all dirty on this filthy hike in the filthy woods," Tandy said.

"Water will cure all your dirt," Kaybee said.

Dave was striding up beside Redwing, asking him all sorts of Indian questions. Jeffrey was attempting to keep up, darting from rock to rock like he was secretly tracking them.

Redwing stopped us in a wide open area without many trees.

"Here," said Redwing extending his arms, "is where our people camped and lived for many years. If you dig down into this soil, you will find arrowheads and pieces of

21

pottery and fish bones. Like this." Redwing took his long knife out of its sheath and dug down into the earth. Soon he held up a broken piece of pottery, round and smooth on one side. Everyone gasped.

"Artifacts are easy to find, especially at this spot," Redwing said. "This was their garbage dump. You'll have time to dig here later. Follow me." He moved us up the trail.

Over to my right, Carmen tapped Pinky on the shoulder. "So," Carmen said, "Judy, my roommate, left. Who am I going to move in with?"

"Not me," Pinky said. "Tandy is plenty of roommate for me."

What a pain, I thought. I wondered if Pinky had one kind bone in her whole body.

"Carmen," I said, "you can move in with Kaybee and me. Right, Kaybee?"

"Certainly," Kaybee said with a grin. "The tent is our world, and there's room aplenty in our world for you."

Carmen rolled her eyes. "Oh, great."

"Not me," large Vince said, wheezing his way up the hill. "No, sir, not a rough boy like me. *I'm* not afraid to camp out alone. My tent partner left, too, but am I begging for company? Not me. Boys like me don't need a roommate."

"That's right," Carmen said to Vince. "You're fat enough to be your *own* roommate."

Everybody's laughter echoed up and down the hill. Vince didn't say anything. I guess he was used to jokes about his weight.

Redwing moved us onward through the dark green forest. At the top of the hill the evergreen trees were huge and the ground was cushioned with pine needles like a padded carpet.

22

We took a ▮▮▮ down to the marshy end of the lake where we got glimpses of huge bullfrogs and long black snakes. We followed the shoreline around to where Redwing had his camp and everyone got to look inside his teepee. He had a television set in there!

Next we walked through another artifact zone, where Redwing said the Indians hunted and camped in winter. Then we followed the stream down around behind our tents, and when we arrived back at the trading post, which stood across the road from the lodge, we were all dead on our feet.

"I have to go lie down," Tandy whined.

"Don't forget the canoe lessons in a half hour," I called after her.

"Gwen!" Jeffrey said, bouncing up to me. "Did you see all the neat stuff in the trading post? You can buy moccasins and T-shirts and all sorts of junk. There's even a museum in there with lots of Indian autofacts."

"*Arti*facts, Jeffrey."

"Yeah! You coming?"

"I'm not going anywhere with you," I said coolly. "You hit me in the face with a french fry, Jeffrey."

"Yeah," he said, "Flicked you on the nose, right? Left a dot of ketchup there, like a zit."

I started to smile against my will. "It's not funny."

"I didn't mean to do it, Gwen. Honest. I'm really sorry."

"Okay," I said. "Apology accepted."

He grinned. "I really meant to hit you with a hamburger!"

"Jeffrey!" I punched him in the arm.

"Only kidding!" he said. "Hey, it's weird about your book, huh?"

"It sure is, J.M. Who do you think took it?"

23

"Beats me," he said, chuckling. "Al Nerd sure did think it was funny, though.

"A real gut-buster, Jeffrey. Wish I knew who stole it, I'd—"

"Let's talk about it later, okay? I want to get over to the trading post."

"Sure, J.M. I think I'll just sit out by the lake. See you later." Jeffrey hustled off. I was glad he was my friend again.

I went through the front door of the lodge and headed toward the back patio. But when I looked to my left, I stopped. There, sitting at the desk in the counselor's office, was Ellie Nord. Her head was bent over a thick paperback book.

It couldn't be, I thought. I turned and slowly walked toward her. No, it couldn't be.

"Hi, Mrs. Nord," I said.

"Hi, Gwendolyn," she said.

"Excuse me, but what are you reading?"

She smiled. "*Gone with the Wind*. I found it lying here on the desk and just couldn't resist."

"On the desk?" I said. "What was it doing there?"

Ellie looked puzzled. "What do you mean?"

"Didn't you hear? That's my book. Someone *stole* it from my tent a little while ago."

"What?" Ellie exclaimed. "Are you sure? I thought maybe someone left it in the other room and Al brought it in here."

I shook my head. "No. I'm certain I left it in my tent."

Ellie sighed. "I thought the boys might retaliate after the food fight. I wonder who took your book."

"I don't know, but I'll bet your husband ends up blaming the girls." I blushed immediately. "Oh, I'm sorry, I didn't mean to—"

Ellie waved her hand and smiled. "It's okay. Al is always sticking up for the boys. He thinks he's macho!"

We laughed. "Well, thanks for holding on to my book. You might as well keep it for a while. You can read it while I'm canoeing. I'd better get going."

"Thanks, Gwen," Ellie said. "And I hope you catch the thief!"

On the back porch of the lodge were some redwood chairs facing the sparkling lake. I sat and gazed out over the peaceful water. It was terrific being away from home and on my own.

Al Nord walked by.

"I found my book," I said. "It was in your office."

He smiled and shook his head. "Yup, a typical gag. Well, I'm glad that's over. See you later."

No wonder the guys call him Nerd, I thought.

"Hi, Gwen." It was Kaybee. She had changed into her bathing suit, a one-piece red one with blue elephants on it. Elephants on a bathing suit? Oh, well. That's Kaybee Keeper for you.

Kaybee dragged over another chair and sat beside me. "I'm happy you found your book."

"Thanks. How are you doing?" I asked. "Like it here?"

She shrugged. "It's better than prison. But I'm mega-scared, Gwen. The kids will be making fun of my sports the whole weekend."

"Oh, don't worry about the sports, Kaybee. Just do your best, enjoy it."

"I will try. But others will not enjoy my trying."

Crunch McFink stomped up. I decided to be nice to him to keep the peace.

"Hi, Crunch," I said, smiling.

"Eat slime," he barked.

"Ooshy gracious!" Kaybee said. "No slime for me, please."

"This stinking camp stinks," Crunch grumbled.

"You don't like it here?" I asked.

"The food fight was okay, but the rest stinks. Hey, what am I talking to you for? I just came over because Nerd told me to tell you to get to the sissy canoe docks."

"Already!" I said. "I haven't changed yet!" I rushed to my tent to slip into my bathing suit. By the time I got to the docks, Redwing was already taking canoes off their racks, ignoring everything that was going on.

"Now listen," Al Nord said. "I'm going to teach you how to use a canoe *safely*. It's easy, but you have to do it right."

He showed us how to get in a canoe without tipping it over and how to kneel correctly. Then he showed us how to paddle using a "J" stroke—paddle straight back and end with a hook action. If you tip over, Al Nord said, hang onto the canoe because it won't sink.

"Okay," he finally said. "Get a partner and let's go canoeing. Remember, be safe. And *never* stand up."

Fat Vince walked up to Al Nord. "I don't have a partner."

"Me, either," Carmen said.

"So, what's the problem?" Al Nord said. "Go together."

"Terrific," Carmen said. "Okay, let's go, blimp. I just hope you don't sink us."

We all had to put on bright orange life vests. They looked bulky, but once you had them on you hardly knew they were there.

Jeff and Dave were the first ones into a canoe. Their eyes were sparkling and their lips were curled into little smiles. I figured they were playing Indian again.

Kaybee and I managed to enter our canoe without tip-

26

ping it. Off we went, smoothly gliding through the water. It was a terrific feeling.

"Is the lake deep?" Kaybee asked.

"Probably," I replied.

"Hmmmm," Kaybee said. "I wonder what it would be like to live deep down there in a water world where everything is wet."

"Let's not find out, okay?"

Soon we were all out on the lake. Every once in a while, we'd see a fish swim by, probably wondering what on earth we were.

"Left! No, no, right!" It was Mack who was yelling. He was sharing a canoe with Crunch, and they were going around and around in a circle out in the middle of the lake. Kaybee and I giggled. Soon they figured out how to paddle straight, and off they zoomed.

"Stop moving!" Carmen screamed.

With Vince in the back, the front of their canoe was tilted up so much it looked like they were going to take off for the moon.

"Okay, okay," Vince said nervously.

"Now paddle!" Carmen ordered. And they were off.

Soon Crunch and Mack floated up beside Pinky and Tandy.

"You weaklings having fun?" Crunch mocked.

Pinky was angry immediately. "Weaklings, huh? How about a race?"

"No," Tandy said. "I don't wanna race." She was obviously scared, and clung hard to the sides of the canoe.

"Shut up, wimp," Pinky said. "There are canoe races tomorrow, so we might as well practice."

"And you need it." Crunch laughed. "You want a race, you got one. Ready, Mack?"

Mack shrugged. "Why not."

27

"Get set, Tandy," Pinky said. "Get that paddle in the water. All you have to do is stroke hard. And I mean *hard!*"

"I'll try," Tandy said quietly.

"Ready?" Pinky asked.

"All set," Crunch replied. He and Mack had their paddles over the water, ready to plunge in.

"Go!" Pinky yelled.

It happened so quickly that if I hadn't been looking I would have missed it.

Crunch paddled before Mack did, and he paddled hard. The front of their canoe smashed into Pinky's, right where Tandy was sitting. Tandy screamed and stood up, then started to lose her balance.

"Oh! Oh!" Tandy rocked back and forth, waving her arms like she was trying to fly.

Then Pinky stood up, too. She reached forward to grab Tandy, but lost her balance. Both girls shrieked and, like trees, tipped over the side and fell into the water.

From the shore, Al Nord began yelling. "Crunch! Let them grab your paddle! Grab his paddle, girls! Grab the canoe! Don't panic!"

Al Nord was going to jump in after them, but Pinky and Tandy, bobbing along in the life vests, grabbed the side of their canoe, kicked their feet, and swam all the way to shore.

"Everybody in!" Al Nord called.

Tandy crawled out of the water, soaked like a rat and crying her eyes out. "They did it on purpose! They tried to kill us!"

"It was an accident!" Crunch yelled, running up.

"Honest!" Mack said.

Pinky, who had some brown slimy stuff in her hair,

started screaming. "They meant to do it! Kick them out of camp!"

Soon the rest of the kids were on shore, and Redwing was calmly putting away the canoes.

Al Nord said, "I saw the whole thing. Your first mistake, Pinky, was goading the boys into a race. But your biggest mistake was standing up in your canoe. I told you the safety rules, and you broke them."

"I don't *believe* it!" Pinky yelled. "I'm getting blamed *again!*"

"Who else is at fault?" Al Nord asked. "Crunch and Mack because they didn't know how to race a canoe? Pinky, Tandy, you remain here with me to go over the safety rules again. The rest of you, beat it. Be back at three o'clock for frog catching."

The boys were laughing as they walked away, which really got me mad. I went with the girls back to my tent, where we sat and talked until Pinky and Tandy finally arrived. Tandy was still sniffling.

"Are you all right?" I asked.

"No, I'm not all right," Tandy cried. "Crunch and Mack tried to kill me. I hate them!"

"And I'm sick of Al Nord always taking the boys' side," Pinky said. "They'll be sorry."

"Pinky," I said. "Causing even more trouble isn't going to help at all."

"Listen, Gwen, I'm not going to just sit here and take the blame for all the trouble," Pinky said.

"Nobody's blaming you for *all* the trouble," I said. "What about my book? You're not to blame for stealing that. I'll bet one of the boys is the thief, and if we can find him Al Nord will have someone else to yell at."

All the other girls seemed to think this was a good idea. Except Pinky.

29

"Who cares about your idiotic book, anyway? Those guys are making me look like a real jerk, and I'm not going to stand for it. And, Gwen, I'm sick of you trying to turn us into one big happy family. Get off my back, will you?"

"Yeah," Tandy said, "get off our back."

I held my tongue. Maybe I was being too bossy. At any rate, I sure wasn't helping the situation.

"Now what?" Carmen asked. "We're fighting with each other, fighting with the boys, fighting to win the games, and fighting to find this sneak thief. What is this, the C.I.A. training camp?"

"Hopping hippos!" Kaybee yipped. "I have a brainsome idea!"

"You do?" Carmen said, astonished.

"Yes. I have been reading about it in a science fiction book. A small group of Blue Aliens are visiting Earth. Everything is peaceful until the president of the United States vanishes! A group of mean Earthmen blame the Blue Aliens and set out to kill them. But the Blue Aliens are innocent! So, the aliens must think fast to save their lives—and they get a zapping good idea! They make an android that looks exactly like the president, then they announce that they've found him! They are made heroes, and the mean Earthmen are sent to intergalactic jail. I don't know what happens next, because I'm still reading the book."

Pinky laughed. "That's very entertaining, Kaybee, but it's stupid. What's it got to do with us?"

"Oh, Pinky, open your eyes and think," Kaybee said. "The mean boys are treating us like Blue Aliens. They are out to get us, and we are helpless. So, somehow, we must trick them. We must turn our trouble into a good thing for us and a bad thing for them."

30

Pinky tapped her forehead and closed her eyes. "Hold it. Hold it. You're wacky, Kaybee, but I think there might be an idea there somewhere. Yes, I've got it!"

"What? What?" Carmen and Tandy asked Pinky.

Pinky smiled widely, rubbed her hands together and whispered: "*Sabotage*. Blue Alien sabotage!"

Jeff

ALL the guys thought the sight of Pinky and Tandy flying over the edge of their canoe and splashing into the lake was the funniest thing we'd ever seen.

"We've gotta think up something else to do to the girls," Crunch said. "This is great."

"Al Nerd is getting mad," Dave said.

"So what?" Crunch said. "Who cares? It's the girls he always gets mad at!"

"Funny how that happens," I said.

"Frogs!" said Mack. He pointed to his watch. "We're late."

We all ran down to the lake behind the lodge. When we got there, the girls and Al Nerd were waiting.

"Now that we're all here, we can begin," Al Nerd said. "It's very simple. You each get one of these butterfly nets and a plastic pail. You walk around the lake and catch frogs and put them in the pail. You bring the frogs back here—we'll keep the boys' frogs and the girls' frogs separate. Later you'll choose the best frogs for the frog race. Any questions?"

"Yeah," Dave said. "Do we get to eat them after the race?"

Everybody groaned and made throw-up sounds.

"No," Al Nerd said. "And you aren't to hurt them either. All the frogs will be released back into the lake after the race. Any *real* questions? No? Well, hop to it! That's a joke, get it?"

Kaybee giggled, but no one else did.

Dave and I took off around the lake, and we soon discovered that catching frogs wasn't as easy as it sounded. They were fast! Also, some of them we saw were huge, and we were afraid to go near them. Monster frogs, really.

Across the lake, we could see Carmen and Gwen swooshing at the water for frogs. Farther up, we saw Pinky nab Tandy before she fell headfirst into the water. Fat Vince was walking along the shoreline making frog sounds.

About an hour later, Dave and I had three frogs in our pail.

"Jeff?"

"What?"

Dave chuckled. "I've got an idea."

"What?"

"It seems to me we have one extra frog here."

"Brilliant."

"Wouldn't it be funny if, say, Pinky slides into bed tonight and feels something kind of cold and squishy wriggling around her legs?"

"No, Dave, no. No way. Forget it."

"She screams, leaps out of bed, throws back the covers. *Boing!* It's Mr. Frog, come to spend the night!"

"Definitely not! Pinky's already mad. This will turn her into a wild girl."

"Yeah," Dave said, thinking. "Maybe you're right.

34

Look, here comes Mack. Let's ask him. He's a level-headed guy. If he agrees, will you do it?''

''Mack will never agree to it. I know he won't, he's too nice a guy. Okay, you're on. If he agrees, we'll do it.''

''Hey, Mack,'' Dave yelled. ''Come here a second.''

Mack came walking over. He had two frogs in his pail. ''Hi.''

''We've got something to ask you,'' I said.

''Here it is,'' Dave said. ''I want to put a frog in Pinky's bed. Jeff says it'll only start more trouble. What do you think?''

Mack looked at Dave. He looked at me. He looked at his frogs.

''Do it,'' Mack said, smiling.

''I don't believe it!'' I said. ''Mack, you never pull gags. What gives?''

Mack looked at me. ''I don't know. It just sounds like fun.''

''Let's go!'' Dave said.

Before long we were sneaking up behind the girls' tents.

''Looks like the coast is clear,'' Dave said. ''Let's make it fast. Put down your buckets. I'll grab a frog. Let's move!''

Like a SWAT team, we ran low and hard for Pinky's tent. We flattened out on the side, then slid around to the front. Dave made a motion, and we burst in through the flaps. The tent was empty.

''This must be Pinky's cot,'' Dave said.

''Let's do it,'' Mack said.

Dave slid the squirmy frog deep down between the sheets.

''Wait till she finds that!'' Dave said.

''She already has!''

We spun around. Pinky was standing in the entrance to

35

her tent. "You are the dumbest three guys I've ever known. I saw you from way down by the lake sneaking up here. And boy, are you jerks in trouble now."

Dave started laughing nervously. "Hey, Pinky, I'm sorry. It was my idea. I thought it would be harmless fun, you know? I'll just take the frog and get out of here."

"Leave the frog," Pinky said. "I didn't bother to catch a frog down by the lake. I'll just take this one."

I was surprised how calm Pinky was acting about this whole thing.

"Now get out of here," Pinky said.

We scrambled out of the tent.

"I don't get it," Dave said. "She didn't even yell."

"Yeah, and after all the trouble she's been blamed for," I said.

We turned in our frogs and sat down by the trading post. Soon, from the girls' tents, we heard someone scream: "Yaaa! Who put a frog in my bed!" It was Gwen.

"Oh, no," Dave said.

Then we heard Pinky: "It was those boys, Gwen. Dave, Jeff, and Mack. I caught them in my tent trying to do the same thing to me. They must have got you, too! Let's go tell Al Nord!"

"We didn't put a frog in *Gwen's* bed," I said.

"No, we didn't," Mack said.

It wasn't hard to figure out who had.

Pretty soon Al Nerd walked up to us, waving a frog in our faces. With him were Gwen, Pinky, and the rest of the smirking girls. "You boys just *had* to get back at the girls, didn't you?"

"I, we, um," I said.

"It was sabotage!" Dave said. "See, we went up there and—"

Al Nerd shook his head and smiled. "Do you know how

36

old this trick is? Everybody does it. And because you were so stupid and definitely not original, I want you to apologize.''

"Sorry," Dave and Mack and I mumbled together.

Al Nerd walked off with the frog croaking in his hand.

"Ahhhh," Pinky said. "Revenge feels great. Chalk one up for the Blue Aliens. Right, Kaybee?''

Kaybee raised her hand and gave Pinky an upside down OK sign, then left with Gwen, who was mad mostly at me.

"Okay, Pinky," Dave said, "you got back at us. We're sorry. Now we're even, right?''

Pinky just grinned, then she, Carmen, and Tandy left.

"Great idea, Dave," I said.

"It's was Mack's fault!" Dave said.

Mack looked at him and said, "Frogs," then just shook his head and left.

Soon it was time for dinner.

Happy and Otto Asterman cooked a feast of roast beef, mashed potatoes, corn, and pumpkin pie. Al and Ellie Nerd stood guard over us to make sure we wouldn't launch any more food into orbit.

After dinner was the frog race. Everybody was excited, except the frogs.

"Each boy picks a frog," said Al Nerd, "and each girl picks a frog. We'll hold them down on that line, about twenty feet from the edge of the lake. When I say 'Go,' release your frog. The first frog into the water wins.''

"I'd still rather eat mine," Dave said.

I smacked him. "Cut that out. We don't want to give Happy and Otto any ideas.''

The frogs squirmed and kicked when we tried to pick them up. Other than that, they were pretty friendly.

"I'm not touching those disgusting things," Tandy said.

37

"They won't hurt you," Ellie Nerd said.

"But they're so ugly and slimy," Tandy whined.

Ellie reached into her back pocket and pulled out a pair of work gloves. "Here, Tandy, wear these."

"Okay," Tandy said.

"What a wimp," Pinky said.

"All frogs to the line!" Al Nerd called.

We each brought our frog down to the line drawn in the sand.

"My frog's a boy frog," Vince said. "He's macho. No girl frog in the world can beat him."

"Oh, yeah?" Pinky said. "Well, my frog's a mass murderer, so keep your stupid macho frog away!"

Everybody laughed.

"All set?" Al Nerd asked.

"Yes, just hurry up," Tandy said. Her arm was stretched out as far as it could go, holding her frog down toward the line.

"Ready . . . set . . . go!"

Immediately Tandy screamed and ran away. She had been holding her frog backwards and it had jumped right at her.

All the other frogs took about two hops, then just sat still, checking out where they were and where they were going.

Gwen's frog inched forward. Mine took a good leap and was in the lead until Carmen's frog kind of crawled ahead of mine.

"Go! Go!" Carmen yelled.

"Crank up those legs!" Dave said to his lazy frog.

Ga-dump. Ga-dump. Ga-dump.

Little by little, the frogs were leaping their way toward the water. Pinky's hopped ahead, then Gwen's took the

38

lead. Finally, Kaybee's frog moved for the first time and jumped sideways.

They were now about eight feet from the water.

"Go! Come on! Move it!" We were really into it.

Pinky's frog turned around and started hopping back toward her. "No, you stupid green jerk! The *other* way!"

"I can't believe it!" Vince said. His frog was still on the start line, sitting there bulging its neck in and out.

"Some macho frog you've got there." Carmen laughed. "Hey, mine's almost to the water!"

Sure enough, Carmen's frog was only about two feet from the water, and a good three feet ahead of everybody else's.

"Hit the gas!" I screamed at my frog.

"I'm gonna win! I'm gonna win!" Carmen screamed.

Suddenly, without warning, Vince's frog croaked so loudly that it scared everybody. Ga-dump. It took a leap. Ga-dump. Ga-dump. It took two more huge leaps. Ga-dump-ga-dump-ga-dump. Now it was in second place, about a foot behind Carmen's.

Fat Vince was going bananas. "Go, you macho frog! Hop! Jump! Leap your way into the record books!"

Ga-dump. Vince's frog hopped one more time—right smack on the back of Carmen's frog.

"Hey!" Carmen yelled.

Carmen's frog was struggling to go, but Vince's frog wouldn't let it. They sat that way for a minute, kind of looking around.

"That's cheating!" Carmen said.

"Frogs can't cheat," I said.

Then, with one more big croak, Vince's frog flew into the air. Splash.

"I won! I won! I won!" Vince yelled, rolling around on the ground like a sea lion.

39

"The boys are victorious again!" Dave said.

"Right!" I said, carried away by the victory. "We won volleyball, and now frogs. We're ahead, two games to zip."

"We're gonna do a clean sweep," Vince said. "We're gonna win every single event! We're great! We're guys! We're great guys!"

"Sorry, girls," Al Nerd said, "the boys win, fair and square." He left to dump the rest of the frogs in the lake.

Carmen pointed her finger at Vince. "This is the last event you guys are going to win."

"Carmen's right," Gwen said. "In the rest of the events a frog can't win for you. You'll have to beat us, and we're going to be ready."

Vince chuckled. "How can you hope to beat tough guys like us?"

"There's more than one way to win," Pinky said. "Be ready for anything boys, and I mean *anything*."

Carmen and Pinky stormed off.

"Sore losers," Vince called after them. "You'd think they'd be used to it by now."

"And you're a sore winner!" Kaybee said. She, too, left. Tandy followed right behind her.

Gwen was left alone with us guys.

"Listen," Gwen said to us, "you don't have to be so hard on us. You know what a temper Pinky has."

"Tough," Vince said. "It's called the spirit of competition. You've gotta give one hundred and ten percent to win. If you can't take it, lump it."

Gwen said, "I have a feeling, fellas, that you are the ones who will be feeling the lumps. Don't say I didn't warn you." And after one more hard glare at Vince, Gwen left.

Al Nerd returned. "You've got fifteen minutes to get ready for the campfire. Try to stay out of trouble, okay?"

"Sure. Yeah. You bet," we all said.

Al and Ellie Nerd left.

"You know," Dave said. "Maybe we *should* take it easier on the girls. We sure would all have more fun."

"Are you kidding?" Vince said. "I'm having fun now!"

"Me, too," Crunch said. "How about you, Mack?"

"The time of my life," Mack said.

Oh, well, I thought. At least we can all look forward to the campfire. Nothing much can happen at a campfire, can it?

Gwen

THE sky was starting to get dark when we arrived at the campfire area at the west end of the lake. The boys weren't there yet. Al and Ellie Nord sat close together on a log beside the huge fire that was already crackling in a beautiful clearing in the dense woods. The white smoke spiraled up through the thick leaves and disappeared into the darkening gray-blue sky.

"The heavens will open their stars soon," Kaybee said, looking up. "But this starless sky is also mega-lovely. You know, Gwen, I am beginning to like the daytime almost as much as the nighttime."

"Why?" I asked.

"Well, at night, all you can see is darkness. If you want to see anything, you must go look up at the stars. But during the day, you can see all the glories around you—except the stars, of course. It is a very brilliant arrangement."

"Yes, it is," I said. Kaybee really thought in interesting ways.

For the first time since I'd been at camp, I took time to

43

relax. The woods were peaceful and smelled of plants and moss and all sorts of living things. It seemed strange to me that humans chose to live in cities instead of out here in the open with nature.

The other girls must have been sharing my good feelings.

"I like this," Tandy said to no one in particular. "The fire smells wonderful, and my bug spray is working."

"Ahh," Carmen said after taking a deep breath. "Paradise."

"Yes," Pinky agreed. "Life out here in the woods totally without creepy boys. Paradise."

We all laughed. Then, our mood was shattered when the boys arrived.

"Where are the marshmallows?" huge Vince said. "A campfire is nothing without marshmallows. I sure hope we're having marshmallows. We are having marshmallows, aren't we?"

"Are we having marshmallows?" Crunch asked Al Nord, who was poking at the fire with a long stick.

"Sorry, no marshmallows," he said.

"Geez," Vince huffed. "I'm still hungry."

"Why don't you eat a tree or something, fatso," Carmen said. As usual, Vince ignored her remark.

We all sat in a circle around the fire, staring like zombies at the dancing flames. As the night got darker, it also got cooler and the warmth of the fire felt good.

Al Nord clapped his hands. "To get us in the proper mood, my wife, Ellie, is going to lead us all in a song. Ellie?"

"I'm not singing," Crunch said firmly.

"Aw, come on, Crunch," Vince said. "If this big guy can sing, so can you." Vince cleared his throat and started singing la-las to warm up. I didn't like him much, but I had to laugh.

44

"Does everybody know 'Row, Row, Row Your Boat'?"
Ellie asked.

"Yeah," Pinky said, "we learned it in the third grade."

"Good," Ellie said, "now you can sing it properly.
And we'll sing it in rounds."

She told us that two people would begin singing, then
two more would start a few measures later, and so on.
We'd all done this before, and once we started singing it
sounded really good.

Our voices filled the forest, and everybody, including
Crunch and Pinky, were soon singing their hearts out. Fat
Vince rocked back and forth, belting out the song louder
than anyone in the worst singing voice I'd ever heard. But
he was having so much fun, he helped everyone else have
fun, too.

After we sang a few more songs the breeze picked up and
we moved closer to the fire. It was definitely nighttime
now, and all our faces glowed orange in the light from the
campfire.

Dave sniffed. "You smell something burning?" he asked
me.

I sniffed. "Yes. And it's not just the fire."

Jeffrey sniffed. "Smells like rubber."

"Your sneakers!" Vince yelled at Jeffrey.

Jeffrey yanked his feet back from the fire edge. The
bottoms were smoking with thick black smoke. "Holy
cow!"

Quickly, Al Nord rubbed dirt onto the bottoms of Jeffrey's sneakers. "Wow, they're melted. Didn't you feel
anything?"

"Nope," Jeffrey said, looking at his smooth sneaker
bottoms. "Wow. And I had them near the fire for only a
minute."

Dave made a few hot-foot jokes and everybody laughed. Then Redwing appeared in the light of the campfire.

"Welcome, Redwing," Al Nord said. "Kids, Redwing is here to tell you a story about the Indians."

"How?" Dave said, laughing hard at himself.

Redwing ignored him and just stood stone-still until everyone was quiet. It was pitch-black night now, and all we could hear was the crackling fire and the hoot of a distant owl.

Jeffrey was excited and he smiled at me. I smiled back.

"A long time ago," Redwing began, "a legend was born in this very Indian camp. A chief was killed by a bear, but all the tribe found was blood on the forest floor. Neither the chief's body or the bear was ever seen again. The Indians believed that their chief's spirit merged with the bear's, and that they became the guardian spirit of this forest. They believed that if any danger or evil people came to these sacred grounds, the spirit would rise up to protect the noble tribe."

"Yeah, sure," Vince whispered.

"Shut up," Mack said to him. Mack, I could tell, was scared.

"Even to this day," Redwing continued, "the spirit that guarded my ancestors still roams this very forest. No evil has thrived here in uncountable moons. This, I tell you, is the truth."

"This, I tell you, is garbage." Dave snickered.

Tandy moved a little closer to me, shivering with fear.

"Do not make fun!" Redwing boomed. "I *know* this to be the *truth*. For I, Redwing, have personally seen the Spirit of the Forest. And . . . I saw it . . . *last night*."

"Last night?" Mack whispered.

The cool breeze turned into a stronger wind and whirled around the campfire scattering sparks.

46

"The spirit," Redwing went on, "only appears when great evil invades its land. You, you, and you—all of you children, have been causing trouble here. Now, the Spirit of the Forest has returned, ready to strike out if necessary. But before it does that, it always leaves a warning."

"W-what kind of warning?" Crunch asked.

The fire flickered in Redwing's black eyes. "You will know it when it happens. Believe me." He looked hard at Vince.

Vince gulped loudly.

Tandy grabbed my arm.

Jeff's mouth fell open.

We were all so frightened we couldn't move.

Suddenly, Redwing turned and silently slid into the dark depths of the forest.

"What a weirdo," Carmen said, pretending not to be scared.

"Wow," Mack whispered. "That was worse than the ghost stories my grandfather used to tell—because the ghost could really be *here*."

The forest rustled with a gust. A light rain began to fall.

"Redwing believes certain things," Al Nord said. "Old things. The Indians are full of legends, and behind each one, you will always find a certain amount of truth if you look."

"*I'm* not looking," Mack said.

"I am," Kaybee said, who was flat on her back. "I am looking at the raindrops drop on my eyeballs."

With a great burst of relief, everybody had a good laugh.

"Better close your eyes, Kaybee," Pinky said. "Here comes a waterfall!"

Like a million buckets in the sky suddenly tipped over, the rain came streaming down.

"Everybody to the lodge!" Al Nord yelled.

The fire hissed and spat as the rain pelted its red-hot embers. We scrambled to our feet and took off down the muddy trail. When we reached the lodge, all of us were soaked to the bone.

Ellie Nord already had a fire going inside.

"Everybody take off your wet sneaks and line them up by the fire," Al Nord said. "But not too close."

"Yeah," Dave said, "remember the freaky legend of fire-foot Jeff!"

Everybody cracked up. Otto and Happy brought in mugs of hot chocolate, and by the time we finished drinking the rain had almost stopped.

"Better leave your sneakers here tonight to dry," Al Nord said. "Watch where you step on the way back to your tents. I'll leave the trail lights on until you get there. See you in the morning."

We all walked up toward the tents together, not saying too much. We grunted "good night" to the boys, and they mumbled "see ya" to us. Soon after we got back to our tents, chaos broke out.

"Someone tied all our clothes together!" Pinky yelled.

"It looks like a big clothes rope!" Kaybee said.

"Look!" Tandy yelped. "My toothpaste and soap and powder are *inside* my socks!"

"Hey, those are *my* socks!" I screamed.

I was fuming. Somehow, someway, the boys had to have done this. This was the last straw.

"Come on, girls," I said. "I think it's time we had a chat with the creeps."

With thin lips and mean frowns, we grabbed a couple of flashlights and stomped through the drizzle to the boys' tents, ouching and ooing in our bare feet.

"Jeffrey! Dave! Crunch! All you guys!" I yelled. "We want to talk with you. *Now!*"

To my surprise, Jeffrey burst out of his tent and came right toward us. The rest of the boys were right behind him.

"And we want to talk to you!" Jeffrey said.

"Yeah, what's the big idea!" Vince yelled.

"We don't know how you did it," Crunch said, "but we don't like it!"

"What are you yapping about?" I asked.

"You tied all our clothes together!" Dave said.

"What!" I shrieked. "Someone tied all *our* clothes together, too!"

"WHAT?" all the boys said.

Redwing and Al Nord came running up. "What's all the noise?" Al Nord asked.

"Someone tied all our clothes together, both us and the boys," I said.

"What!" Al Nord said.

Redwing just stood there, shaking his head back and forth.

"I'm beginning to get tired of these gags," Al Nord said. "I want to know who did this."

"You may never know," Redwing said in a low, quiet voice.

"Huh?" Al Nord said. "Do you know who it is?"

Redwing nodded slowly. "Yes. I know. This is the warning I spoke about."

"Oh, you're crazy," Vince huffed.

"I am not," Redwing said. "We were all at the campfire. Who could have done this strange thing? Who would do it to *everyone?* Believe me. The Spirit of the Forest has left his warning. *Beware.*"

And with that, Redwing turned around and walked off.

49

No one knew what to say. It was too strange.

Al Nord simply said, "Go to bed," and he left.

"I'm scared," Tandy whined.

"Don't worry," I said, "we all are. What a horrifying story."

"Ghosts! Ha!" Vince bellowed. "Big joke. That jerk Redwing is pulling something, but I'm not going to fall for it, and I'm sure the other guys aren't going to either. Maybe you sissy girls are afraid, but *I'm* sure not."

"Crunch," Mack said. "Let's go back together, okay?"

Crunch laughed. "Gee, I feel like a babysitter. Okay, punk, let's go." They left.

"Vince," Jeff said, "you can bunk with Dave and me if you want to. I mean, no sense in staying alone if you don't have to."

"No sweat," Vince said, with rain dribbling down his piggy face. "This boy can handle it on his own. Girls, if any of you get scared, come on over. I'll protect you from the big bad ghost."

"I'd rather die first," I snapped. "Why don't you slither back to your cave."

With a wave and smile, Vince left.

"I don't like that fat guy," I said. I was furious.

"He sure does think boys are the best thing in the world to be," Kaybee said. And she began to walk away with the rest of the girls.

"Hey, Gwen," Jeffrey called. "Come here a minute."

"It's raining out, J.M." I said. My hair was a mop.

"You know who could be behind this gag?" he whispered.

"Who?"

"Mack."

"*Mack?* Jeffrey, Mack doesn't pull practical jokes."

"Wrong-o," he said.

50

Jeffrey explained to me how he, Dave, and Mack were caught by Pinky and that she put the frog in my cot.

"I know she did," I said. "Kaybee told me. It's part of Pinky's sabotage plan to get back at you guys. Hmmm, Mack wanted to pull the frog joke, eh? Maybe he's the one who took my book, too."

"Possibly."

"And possibly not," I said. "It seems to me that *everybody* is a suspect. We need evidence, Jeffrey. This is turning out to be a major mystery." I shivered. "I'm going to dry off. See you tomorrow."

"Right."

When I got back to my tent, Kaybee was wrapped up tight in two blankets.

"Oh, Gwen, I'm glad you are here," she said.

"You don't believe that ghost tale, do you?"

"Gwen, you know me. I believe the most fantastical of all things in the universe."

I chuckled. I really liked that strange girl.

Just when I was settling into my nice warm bed, Pinky and the rest of the girls burst into our tent.

"Mind if we visit?" Pinky said.

"Do we have a choice?" I asked.

"No," Carmen replied. "We have an idea."

"But first," Pinky said to me, "who do you think tied all our clothes together?"

"I don't know what to think," I said. "It's confusing. We were all at the campfire."

"I vote for Vince," Kaybee said. "He hates girls more than Martian woofmen hate the squirrelwomen."

We all looked at Kaybee and shook our heads.

"Well, we don't know anything for sure," I said. "I wish we could show those guys. If we could just win one event."

51

"That's our idea," Carmen said. "A sure-fire way to win the next event."

"What's coming up tomorrow?" I asked. "Here it is. The first thing is the rope bridge. How can we beat the boys at crossing the rope bridge?"

"I'll tell you," Pinky said. "The campfire gave me the idea. It's perfect. And there's only one person no one will suspect."

"Who?" Carmen asked.

Pinky smiled. "Tandy."

"Me!" Tandy cried.

"Yes, you," Pinky replied. Then she whispered: "Tandy, I want you to go down to the lodge."

"Now? It's raining!"

"Pinky," I said, "we're asking for big trouble."

"Quiet," Pinky said. "It'll work. Trust me. Now, Tandy, go down to the lodge. If Al Nord sees you, tell him you need another blanket or something. But when the coast is clear, sneak quickly over to the fireplace and . . ."

Jeff

I WAS having a great dream. I was flying up over the treetops toward the blue sky. Then I was zooming down to the forest floor. Then I shot straight up again, then plunged back to the ground. I felt something wet under my legs. I looked down. I was riding a gigantic frog! "RIBBIT!" it croaked, and all the animals of the forest ran for cover. Way way up, I soared. Then down down down. Up up up. Down down down. Up up . . .

Suddenly I was at a horse track. I heard a bugle playing the music to announce the start of the race—

"Jeff!"

My giant frog was at the starting gate with the horses—

"Jeff!"

The bugle kept playing loudly—

"*Jeff!* Wake up! Jeff!"

I opened my eyes and Dave's face filled my vision.

"Dave?" I asked. "What are you doing at a horse race?"

I sat up. I was in my tent at Camp Arrowhead. Still, I heard the bugle playing its rapid music.

Dave laughed. "That's reveille."

"It's what?"

"Rev-e-lee. A bugle playing reveille. It's how they wake up soldiers at an army camp."

"Army camp?" I said.

"Are you awake?" Dave said. "It's a record. Al Nerd is blasting reveille over the loudspeakers to wake us up. Come on, it's seven o'clock. Ten minutes to exercises."

"Geesh."

I sleepily crawled into some clothes. My T-shirt was on backwards, but I didn't care.

"Hey! My sneakers are gone," I said. "Where are my sneakers? Someone stole my sneakers!"

"Shhh, dummy," Dave said. "We left them all down in the lodge by the fire, remember?"

"Oh, yeah," I said.

Dave and I left our tent and stumbled down to the lodge, dodging puddles as we went. We slid into our sneakers, which were dry and kind of stiff, then went out front into the bright sunshine. Most of the other kids were there, half-asleep on their feet. Al and Ellie Nerd were jogging in place and smiling. Al flexed his muscles and Ellie smiled at them.

"Exercise is the most important thing you can do to start the day," Al Nerd said. "And—"

Suddenly it seemed like the ground was shaking under our feet. There, thundering down the hill from the tents, came flabby Vince.

"Hey! Hey!" he was yelling. When he reached us, he couldn't talk until he caught his breath. "Hey! Somebody was in my tent! Somebody stole my whole bag of chocolate kisses!"

"The girls did it!" Crunch said.

"We did not!" Pinky said with a stamp of her foot.

54

"Girls, girls, girls," Al Nerd said. "Girls, why must you cause so much trouble?"

"But—" Pinky said.

"No buts," Al Nerd said. "I can't believe the boys would steal from each other. So, whichever of you girls took Vince's candy, I want you to return it immediately."

No one said anything.

"I'll find out who did it," Vince said. "And then I'll, I'll—"

"What are you going to do, fatso?" Pinky said. "Eat the thief?"

Vince started to say something then stopped. Suddenly he looked really embarrassed.

"Pinky, I don't want to hear a cruel comment like that again," Al Nerd said. "Vince, we'll catch that thief. And that's a promise. Now, is everyone here?"

"Tandy isn't," Ellie said.

"Okay," Al Nerd said. "We won't wait for her. I have an announcement to make before we begin. I'm sorry to tell you that Mack Buster left camp last night."

"What happened?" I asked.

Redwing, who had just come out of the lodge with a piece of toast in his hand, paused to listen.

"Mack came pounding on the lodge door at about midnight," Al Nerd said. "He was very frightened, almost hysterical. He insisted on going right home. So, we called his parents and they picked him up about an hour ago."

"Poor boy," Ellie Nerd said. "I never saw anyone so scared."

"What scared him?" Pinky asked.

"It doesn't matter," Al Nerd said.

"Sure it matters," Dave said. "If it was a mountain lion or something, I want to get out of here, too."

"It wasn't a mountain lion," Al Nerd said. "Okay, I'll tell you. Mack said he saw . . . a ghost."

All the kids gasped.

Down by the lodge, Redwing smiled and nodded, then slowly walked away. I looked over to Gwen, and she had seen spooky Redwing too.

"Now," Al Nerd said, "does anyone know anything about this?"

Surprisingly, Crunch raised his hand. "Maybe," he said. "Mack and I kind of had a fight last night. Anyway, we were both kind of mad at each other. Mack said he was going to sleep in Vince's tent. He left and that was the last I saw of Mack."

"Terrific," Al Nerd said. "Vince, what do you know?"

"Me?" Vince said. "Nothing. Mack never showed up."

Al Nerd shook his head. "I wonder who pulled this stupid trick? Not too funny, is it?"

"Ghosts are never funny," Kaybee said.

"Okay," Al Nerd said. "From now on, nobody camps alone. Vince, I want you to move in with Crunch."

"Turtle and me? Aww, geesh!" Crunch huffed.

"It'll be great!" Vince said to Crunch. "What a team!"

"That's settled," Al Nerd said. "Time for some jumping jacks. Let's go!"

We are started jumping like jerks.

Ten minutes later Tandy came walking down.

"Tandy," Ellie Nerd said, "where were you? You missed all the exercises."

"I'm not doing exercises," Tandy said.

"Why not?"

"If I exercise, I'll get sweaty," Tandy said. "If I get sweaty, I'll have to take a shower—and I am *not* taking another shower in that yukky place. I'll get clean in the lake later.

"Wimpy wimp," Pinky said.

When the exercises were over, all us guys held our noses as we passed Tandy.

"Last one to the showers is a stink bomb!" Dave yelled. And we took off.

After we took showers, changed and ate a huge pancake breakfast, we were ready for another day at Camp Arrowhead. We all met about two hundred yards from the lodge at the rope bridge.

The rope bridge was about one hundred feet long and it spanned a narrow part of Lake Hoppipong. The rope bridge looked like a V, with a thick rope you walk on and two higher ropes, one on each side, that you hold on to. It was suspended about ten feet above the water. It was scary and wobbly.

"I can't wait to see fat Vince try to cross that," Pinky said.

The girls giggled.

"You will see him, all right," Vince said. "And I'll be waiting for you on the other side."

"Now," Al Nerd said, flexing his muscles, "let me show you the correct way of crossing the rope bridge."

Al Nerd climbed the wooden steps up to the rope bridge. He put a hand on the left rope, a hand on the right rope, then he stepped onto the thick rope below them.

"Place one foot in front of the other," he said. "Use your hand ropes only for balance, not for support. If you lean on your hands you will fall over. If you fall over, don't worry. The water is plenty deep and you won't get hurt. You'll only get wet."

Al Nerd walked all the way to the end of the rope bridge, then all the way back. He made it look easy.

"Okay," he said. "Girls first."

Pinky climbed the wooden steps and inched onto the

rope and out over the water. At first, she leaned too much on her right hand. Her feet swayed way out to the left. Soon, though, she got her balance and slowly made it to the end of the rope bridge.

"Do I have to come back?" she called.

"Great job!" Al Nerd said. "No, you don't. Just walk down the steps and come back over the footbridge to your right. Who's next?"

Carmen, who had been silent all morning, suddenly stood. "I'll go." Without hesitating, she walked up the steps, across the rope bridge, and back!

"Terrific!" Al Nerd said.

"I do gymnastics at school," Carmen said proudly.

Gwen made it across, but she didn't come back. Kaybee was scared, but she walked halfway across then somehow crawled the rest of the way. She looked really proud of herself when she came back.

"That was like walking on a thread of air," she said.

Tandy almost made it across. Halfway to the end, a bee buzzed her head and she swatted at it with one hand. Her feet flew out to the left, she screamed, and fell into the water. We laughed and laughed until she finally climbed out.

"Well," Dave said, "you got your bath!"

"Okay, boys," Al Nerd said. "You're up."

Dave was first. He took three steps out onto the rope bridge, slipped, and flopped fanny-first into the water.

Crunch went next. He didn't make it either. Splash.

"Come on, Vince," I said. "I know you can do it."

When Vince stepped out onto the rope, it sagged about three feet. Everybody was trying really hard not to laugh. The big guy made it halfway. Then his feet slipped off the rope. SPLASH! He crawled out of the water like a walrus.

I was last. And I was the worst. Two steps. Splash.

"How did those girls do it?" Crunch asked Vince.

"Luck," Vince said.

Dave was sitting on a stone, emptying water from his sneakers.

"I see why you slipped," I said to him. "Old sneakers. No tread. No grip."

Dave looked at the bottoms of his sneakers. "Hey! These sneakers are new! Now there's no tread!"

"Hey!" Vince said. "My tread is all gone too!"

"Mine, too!" Crunch said. He looked closer. "Hey, they're melted!"

"Yeah!" I said, "They're just like mine!"

"Melted?" Al Nerd said. He took Crunch's sneakers. "Sure does look like it. Jeff, your sneakers melted by the fire last night. What about the rest of you?" Al Nerd turned to the girls. "It's hard for me to believe that *all* the boys had their feet close to the fire, and didn't even notice. Are you girls behind this? Did you somehow melt their sneakers at the lodge late last night? Well?"

Tandy's eyes were bulging and she hid behind Gwen. Pinky just smiled and shrugged.

"She did it," Crunch said.

"If she did, she's in trouble," Al Nerd said. "Now, get out of here, all of you troublemakers. Get set for the hike to the cave." He left.

Pinky raised a fist in the air "The Blue Aliens strike again!"

"The what?" Crunch said.

"Um," Pinky said. "It's our name. Our new team name. The Blue Aliens! Right, girls?"

They all agreed by nodding their heads and saying, "I guess so."

After the girls left, we decided to come up with a name for the boys' team.

"I've got it," Vince said. "The Tough Guys!"

We decided to think about it some more.

In a little while, Redwing led us up the winding trail to the cave. The rocks were jagged around the entrance, and the deep, dark hole looked like a hungry mouth.

"This cave used to be sacred ground to my people," Redwing said. "Here, the medicine man came to heal the sick and wounded. There is also a legend of great treasure hidden far back in the cave. But to this day, no one has ever found it. They say the treasure is cursed, and I believe it because every person who has entered the cave seeking the treasure has never come out alive."

"Gee," Tandy said. "I think I'll just wait outside."

"Wimping out again?" Pinky said.

"Stop saying that!" Tandy screamed. "I'm not a wimp! I'm not!"

"Leave her alone, Pinky." Gwen said. "I think I'll stay outside too."

"Not me!" Dave said. "Let's go, Redwing."

Redwing held up a hand. "We are not going very far into the cave. Just inside the entrance is a large area where the medicine man did his healing. But farther in is danger— bats, rodents, bottomless pits."

"And the curse," Carmen said.

"Yes," Redwing said. "And the curse."

Some of us headed into the darkness. Inside the cave wasn't that exciting. It was just a bare open area with a high ceiling you couldn't even see. The rocks inside were wet, and you could hear dripping coming from someplace. Every step, every word, everything echoed in there. It could drive you bananas if you stayed in there too long.

"Hey-hey-hey," Pinky's voice echoed. "I-I found-found the-the treasure-sure-sure!"

"What?-What?-What?" I said.

60

"The-the treasure-sure!" Pinky said. "I-I have-ave it-it!"

Outside I heard Vince announce. "Hey, everybody, Pinky found the treasure!"

When we came out of the cave, we gathered around Pinky, who had her hands behind her back.

"Where is it? Where's the treasure?" Vince asked.

"It's great!" Pinky said. "And, Vince, I'll bet it's the kind of treasure you'll love the most."

"What is it? What is it?" Vince asked.

Pinky brought a hand around in front of her. "Candy! Your chocolate kisses! The perfect treasure for a fatso!"

Dangling from Pinky's hand was Vince's large bag of candies.

Nobody laughed. Everybody could see that this time Pinky's fat joke really got to Vince. He blushed furiously and dropped his head, then started to walk away.

"Hey, blimp, you forgot your food!" Pinky yelled after him.

"Why don't you just shut the heck up!" Gwen yelled at Pinky. She snatched the candy out of Pinky's hand and handed it to me. "Make sure Vince gets it back, J.M."

"Okay," I said. "Gee, I guess he really *does* mind being fat."

Gwen nodded. "Sure he does. That's why he's so obnoxious all the time. He'd rather have people mad at him than making fun of him."

We watched Vince walk away down the trail, a big guy disappearing among the trees and bushes.

"He pains inside like the fire-eaters of Sparkite. I am sad for him," said Kaybee.

The next voice we heard was Al Nerd's. "Pinky, why don't you tell me how Vince's candy got into that cave."

"I don't know, honest!" she said.

"Even if that's true," Al Nerd said, "why were you so

61

cruel to him? Don't you know jokes like that *hurt* a guy like Vince? I thought even *you* were smart enough to know that. Pinky, I want no more cruel comments out of you. And everybody, I want this thief, and I want him—or her—*bad*.''

As we walked back, Dave tried to cheer us up with a few nutty stunts. What a show-off. And Kaybee loved it. Dave and Kaybee walked to the lodge together, and every now and then Kaybee would burst into giggles at something Dave said. He'd finally found the perfect audience.

We sat around by the lake with some dragonfly blood before we went canoeing and swimming.

"Sure is strange without Mack around," I said.

"Yeah," Crunch said, "I miss him like I miss a bad cold."

"Knock it off, Crunch," Gwen said.

"Shut up, slug-face," he said.

"Eat slime!" Gwen said.

I'd never heard her say anything like that. But she was smiling, and so was Crunch. Must have been a secret joke.

Dave was down by the water, showing Kaybee how to skip rocks.

"Oooooo!" she said about fifty times a minute.

When Dave went up to his tent for something, Kaybee tried to skip rocks but couldn't. She stared at the rock in her hand like she was looking for instructions on it.

Pinky and Carmen were sitting under a tree talking to Tandy. They kept glancing our way like they were plotting something. After a few minutes, Tandy said, "Oh, yeah?" and ran off.

Vince sat down beside Gwen.

"You okay, buddy?" I asked him.

"Oh, sure," Vince said. "It's stupid for me to get mad

at somebody who makes fun of my fat. After all, this boy *is* rather large.''

''Well,'' Gwen said, ''you might be large, but it doesn't look too bad on you at all.''

Vince blushed. ''Thanks.''

''Let's go, kids!'' Al Nerd announced, coming out of the lodge in his swimming trunks, his muscles rippling all over the place.

We all gathered at the shoreline.

''We're missing Tandy again,'' Al Nerd said. ''Anyone seen her?''

''She ought to be back any minute,'' Carmen said, giggling.

''Where is she?'' Al Nerd asked.

Carmen chuckled. ''Tandy said she was tired of Pinky calling her a wimp. So, Pinky told Tandy to prove she's not. So, Tandy said 'How?' So—''

''So,'' Pinky said, ''I told her to prove she's not a wimp by going up and getting that treasure from the cave! So the wimp left!''

''What!'' Al Nerd said.

''She'll never go near that cave,'' Pinky said. ''Not in a million years.''

But ten minutes later, Tandy still hadn't come back.

Fifteen minutes later, Tandy still hadn't come back.

Twenty minutes later, we were all furiously rushing up the forest trail toward the cursed cave.

Gwen

AL Nord called to Redwing, who was unloading the canoes from the racks, and he raced over to join us.

"Tandy has gone up to the cave alone," Al Nord told Redwing as they ran along. "She's got a good head start, so let's move out."

Al Nord was in terrific physical shape, but light-footed Redwing breezed past him and up the hill like Al Nord was standing still.

I couldn't keep up with them, and neither could the rest of the girls except Carmen. She sprinted up, keeping pace with Al Nord.

The guys were even slower than we were. Fat Vince and bulky Crunch were already wheezing behind all of us. Dave was running and cracking jokes beside Jeff, but Jeff looked worried and told Dave to shut up.

"Why'd you tease Tandy into going up to the cave, anyway?" I asked Pinky.

"It was a joke, that's all. I never figured she'd be dumb enough to really do it."

I glared at Pinky. "I wonder who the dumb one *really* is."

We rounded a bend in the trail, and I knew we were almost halfway to the cave. From up ahead I heard Al Nord calling "Tandy! Tandy!"

"I've gotta stop," Vince said from down behind me. "This boy has had it."

I yelled back to him. "Stay there in case Tandy comes back."

Vince, breathing hard, waved to me. "Good idea!"

Crunch stayed with Vince. They both sat on a rock, completely exhausted.

I kept running. My feet and legs were feeling heavier with each step, but I forced myself to move on.

"The cave!" Jeffrey said.

We were there. My heart was pounding hard in my chest. Poor Tandy. Please, oh please, don't let her be in there.

Al Nord and Carmen were waiting for us. Carmen must have taken a shortcut through the bushes because she had red marks all over her legs and she was scratching at them.

Al Nord held up both hands. "Redwing has gone inside," he said.

Just then Redwing's echoing voice boomed out from the mouth of the cave. "Tandy-dy-dy-dy-dy . . ."

I leaned against a tree, breathing hard, with one eye riveted on the cave.

"What if she's not in there?" I asked.

"Well, let's hope not," Al Nord said.

"No, I mean, what if she got lost in the woods or something?"

Al Nord blinked a few times. "I hadn't thought of that, Gwen. You might be right. Okay, kids, we've got to spread out. Go in pairs. Walk back down the trail and see if you see any signs of her. I'll stay here in case Redwing needs help."

We all pushed ourselves to our feet. Carmen and Pinky moved west toward the trail around the far end of the lake. Jeffrey and Dave started back the way we came, saying they'd go down and search up behind our tents in case Tandy doubled back. Kaybee and I headed east. All of us were calling Tandy's name as we parted.

"Losing someone like this is scary," I said to Kaybee.

She nodded. "Yes, but losing yourself is mega-worse. I hope Tandy is okay."

"Me too, Kaybee."

We soon found ourselves on the dirt road that led down past the Indian artifact area. We walked slowly down it, cupping our hands around our mouths and calling for Tandy.

When we came to a stream we stopped.

"Let's follow this stream back toward the lake," I said.

We walked carefully but quickly along the mossy bank of the small, gurgling stream.

"Tandy! Tandy!" I yelled. "Please, Tandy, answer." And she did.

"Help! Help!"

"Where's her voice coming from?" I asked.

"Somewhere toward the lakeside," Kaybee replied excitedly.

"Help!"

"Let's go!" We rushed off.

The stream bank was slippery and my foot shot out from under me and splashed into the water. Kaybee caught my arm before I fell in. Without saying anything, I regained my balance and we were off again. The lake was suddenly before us.

"Help! Help!"

"That way," I said, and we started running.

67

The lake curved down to our left and we followed it. Our feet and calves were soaked, but we didn't stop. Soon the rope bridge came into view.

"There she is!" Kaybee shrieked.

Tandy was out in the middle of the rope bridge, dangling from one arm and kicking her feet in the air.

"Help!" she screamed. And just then she lost her grip and fell down into the water.

Relief swept over me. Tandy was okay. She wasn't in the cursed cave, and she'd be all right.

"Who's that on the rope bridge?" Kaybee asked.

"Huh?" I said.

Tandy was swimming to shore, but out in the middle of the rope bridge someone else was still hanging there.

"Is that a kid?" I asked. Actually, it looked more like a baby.

We were almost to the rope bridge when I finally recognized what was hanging from the thick rope.

"It's Tandy's teddy bear!" I said. "I don't believe it."

Before long, we were sitting on the shore with Tandy, who was soaked and sobbing as I hugged her and told her everything would be all right.

"We thought you were in the cave," Kaybee said.

Tandy shook her head. "I'd never go in there! Even Pinky can't make me go up there. All I wanted to do was hide. But I didn't know where to go. I came over here, I don't know why, and then I saw my teddy hanging from the rope bridge!"

"I'll save him," Kaybee said. She inched her way out on the rope bridge and got Tandy's stuffed bear and brought it back.

"Who put teddy out there, Gwen?" Tandy asked.

"I don't know," I said. "But I'll bet it's the same creep

68

who's been pulling all the sneak-thief pranks around here. Come on, let's go tell the others we found you safe and sound.''

About ten minutes later, we were all sitting down on the back patio area of the lodge. Poor Tandy was shivering, wrapped in a towel and hugging her bear.

"I feel like a three-year-old," Tandy said.

Dave, in one of his rare serious moments, said, "Forget it, Tandy, we all have our secrets. Hey, I used to sleep with a rubber lizard!"

But nothing could cheer Tandy up. She tried to hide in her blanket and started crying.

Al Nord was pacing before us. "I don't want *any* of you to *ever* do *anything* like this *again*," he said. "*Never* go off alone. *Never* put yourself in danger. And *never* dare anybody *else* to do it. I don't know who stole Tandy's bear or the other things, but we are *going* to find out, and you can take my word on *that*."

Ellie Nord, who was standing there in her bathing suit, shook her head. "Tricks that hurt people like this can last forever," she said. "Please, kids, think about other people's feelings, okay?" Then she went to take her seat in the lifeguard chair.

"Now, there's no time for canoeing," Al Nord said. "But if anyone wants to take a swim, go ahead. You've got a half an hour until lunchtime."

Silently, we all went up to change into our bathing suits. Tandy said she wasn't going swimming. I didn't blame her.

When we were in our tent, Kaybee said, "I don't understand."

"What?" I asked.

"Why this sneaky person is stealing then returning what he steals in crazy places." Kaybee's face was dead serious,

69

but she was putting on her elephant bathing suit again. It's hard to be serious when you're talking to someone in an elephant bathing suit, but I tried.

"Have any ideas?" I asked.

Kaybee frowned. "Maybe it is just to be mean. Maybe the sneaky person likes to make other kids look as foolish as a bulldog with rabbit ears on."

I laughed. "I think you might be right. Tandy was trying to keep her teddy bear a secret, I know that. Now everybody knows about it. She's very embarrassed."

"I do not like saying this, Gwendolyn, but do you think Jeffrey could be the one?"

"I doubt it. He's sneaky, but I don't think he can be *this* sneaky. I think Dave is more likely."

"No!" Kaybee said. "David is a tricksome person, yes, but he is nice and would never *steal* for his tricks."

"You really like him, don't you?" I asked.

Kaybee blushed. "I guess. His mind thinks in different places, like mine."

"Come on, let's go take a dip."

"And then we can go swimming?"

I giggled and shook my head at silly, wonderful, weird Kaybee.

When we got to the narrow beach by the lake, Jeffrey was standing on the wooden swimming pier with his arms over his head. "Watch this, Gwen!" He aimed his hands at the water, jumped high, and dove in head first. Not a bad dive, I thought.

"Look out, world!" fat Vince yelled. He jumped off the pier, wrapped his arms around his legs, and did a cannonball that sent waves all the way to the other side of the lake.

"What a monster," Carmen said.

I noticed that Carmen hadn't changed into her suit. "Aren't you going in?" I asked her.

She shook her head. "Too tired. I just want to rest for a while." She sat in a lounge chair and rubbed her scratched-up legs a little, then lay back and closed her eyes.

I tested the water with my toe. Then I jumped off the pier and cannonballed Vince.

"Hey, cut it out!" he bellowed.

"You never know when a Blue Alien will strike," Pinky yelled from shore.

"Guys! Guys!" Vince called. "I've got a name for our team. The Blue Alien Beaters!"

"That stinks," Crunch said. "We don't want a team name that sounds anything like theirs."

"Right," Jeff said. "Let's find a name with 'Earth' in it instead of 'Alien.' "

"Think, think, think!" Vince said, tapping his head. "How about the Blue Earthboys?"

Crunch held his nose. "Stinks."

"The Earth Soldiers," Jeff said.

"No," Crunch said. "Earth Generals."

"Wait," hollered Vince. "The Earth Presidents!"

Jeffrey waved his arms. "The Earth *Kings!*"

"Yeah!" Vince boomed.

"That's it!" Crunch screamed.

Before we knew it, it was lunchtime. We all went up to change out of our suits, then came back down to the cafeteria.

I was sitting with Kaybee, Tandy, and Pinky when Crunch, Vince, and Dave came stomping in chanting, "Earth Kings! Earth Kings! Earth Kings!"

"What's all this?" Al Nord asked, taking a big bite of a sandwich.

"We have names now," Vince said. "The girls are the Blue Aliens. We're the Earth Kings."

"Interesting," Al Nord said.

Just then, Jeffrey came tearing in. "I've been robbed! I've been robbed!"

"Oh, no," Al Nord said, swallowing hard.

"My pajamas are gone! Stolen! Right out of my suitcase!"

"Your pajamas?" Pinky said. She looked at me and Kaybee, then over to Tandy. We all started giggling.

"It's not funny!" Jeffrey said. He whirled around, looking at each of us. "Who did it? Which one of you is the thief? I want my pajamas back."

"What did they look like?" Pinky asked.

"Um, well," Jeffrey said. "It doesn't matter. Mr. Nord, someone stole my pajamas!"

It was obvious that Al Nord was mad. He set down his sandwich and almost crushed it.

"All right," he said. "Everybody grab something to eat then gather at this center table here. We're going to have a talk."

Everybody was soon seated.

"Where's Carmen?" Al Nord asked.

"The last time I saw her," I said, "she was sitting out back."

"You all stay here," Al Nord said. "I'll get her."

In a few minutes, Al Nord came back with Carmen, who was rubbing her eyes and moving kind of slow.

"She fell asleep," Al Nord announced. "Carmen, get yourself a sandwich and sit down with the rest of us."

"I'm not hungry," Carmen said. She bent to scratch her legs.

Al Nord studied her. "Are you feeling all right?"

Carmen shrugged. "I guess not." She rubbed her arm.

72

"What are those marks on your legs and arms?" Al Nord asked.

"I don't know," Carmen said. "But they itch like crazy."

Al Nord called to his wife. "Ellie?"

Ellie Nord came into the cafeteria. "Hi," she said.

"Ellie, I think Carmen needs your help," Al Nord said. Then he said to all of us, "Ellie is a doctor."

"A doctor?" Pinky said, astonished. "Gee."

Ellie took a look at Carmen's legs and arms. Then she felt Carmen's forehead. "Fever," she said. "Looks like poison ivy, and a bad case, too. Come on, Carmen, let's take your temperature and see what we can do." Ellie led Carmen out of the room.

"Poor Carmen," Kaybee said.

"So, Jeff," Pinky said, "you going to tell us what your pajamas look like?"

"You ought to know," Jeff said. "You stole them."

"Did not," Pinky said.

"Okay, everybody quiet down and listen up," Al Nord said. He dragged a chair over in front of our table and sat on it backwards. "Kids, I need your help."

"At what?" I asked.

"At a mystery," Al Nord said. "We have to band together and solve a mystery."

"What mystery?" Vince asked. He was getting interested.

"The mystery of your stolen candy, Vince," Al Nord said. "And all the other things someone has been stealing around here."

"But is it really stealing if the things were returned?" Dave asked.

"It's *still* stealing," Jeffrey said.

"Jeff's right," Al Nord said. "I want all of you to make a peace pact. I want to catch this sneak thief, and we

73

can't do it if anyone is pulling pranks. Certainly you kids must feel strange about these thefts.''

"Why?'' Crunch asked.

"Because the thief is one of you. One of your buddies. Maybe the person you are sharing a tent with.''

Each of us looked at his tentmate. I refused to believe for a second that Kaybee would steal anything from anybody.

Vince took hold of Crunch's arm and shook it. "Talk, Scarface,'' Vince said like a 1930's cop. "Where were you on the night of July twenty-second at nine o'clock?''

Crunch started laughing. "You're a riot, Turtle, a real riot.''

"Or,'' Pinky said, "he's a thief.''

"Me?'' Vince said. "Look at me. Is this innocent face the face of a thief?''

"You're right,'' Pinky said. "It's the face of a gorilla.''

We all laughed.

"So, are you with me?'' Al Nord asked.

We all said that we were.

"Great,'' Al Nord said. "Starting right now, the peace pact is on and the hunt for the thief begins. Lock up your valuables. If you have any jewelry, you can lock it in the safe in my office.''

"This is going to take some brain work,'' Jeffrey said. "Maybe some spy work. I'm going back to my tent right now and search for clues.''

"I'll go with you,'' Dave said.

All the nutty boys suddenly thought they were Sherlock Holmes, and as they left the cafeteria they investigated the tables, the doors, the floor, and one another.

"Archery competition in fifteen minutes,'' Al Nord called after them. "I'll go check on Carmen,'' he said to us, then left.

The girls and I sat and looked suspiciously at one another.

"Whooo's the thief?" Pinky said mockingly. "Puh! The whole thing is stupid. I'm not wasting my time playing detective. I've got this great idea to pull on the guys—you just have to hear it."

"Pinky," I said, "we all agreed to a peace pact, remember?"

"Playing mommy again, Gwen? Listen, what better time to pull a gag than during a peace pact!" she said.

"I'm having nothing to do with it," I said. I left and wandered up to Jeffrey's tent.

He was just coming out. "Hiya, Gwen. What's up?"

"Find any clues?"

"Nothing. But it's strange. I kept my money right beside my pajamas. Why didn't the thief take the money instead of my pajamas?"

"It's obvious, J.M. The thief isn't out to steal things and keep them. This thief is out to make us look stupid."

"Yeah," Jeffrey said. "That's what Dave said, too."

"Where is he, anyway? I thought you two came up here together."

Jeffrey shook his head. "You're suspecting him, aren't you? We're all going to end up suspecting one another and fighting over that, too."

"I know. You're right," I said. Sometimes Jeffrey was pretty smart.

"Come on," he said, "let's go down to the archery range and play Indian."

When we got down to the archery range, most of the other kids were already there. They were grouped around one of the large targets, laughing like crazy.

"What are they laughing at?" Jeffrey asked.

"I haven't the slightest idea. Let's go see."

When the kids saw us coming, they laughed even harder and spread apart to make room for us in front of the target.

I couldn't figure out what was going in—until I saw what was pinned to the target with three arrows.

"Oh, no!" Jeffrey screamed. He was blushing red as a tomato.

There, spread across the target, were Jeffrey's pajamas! His *Dumbo* pajamas.

Frantically, Jeffrey pulled out the arrows and took his Dumbo pajamas off the target.

"Hey, Jeff," Pinky said. "Dumbo sure is macho!"

"Very cute, Jeffrey," Kaybee said. "I like them."

"It's downright embarrassing," Pinky said. "An Earth King who wears Dumbo pajamas."

"Shut up" Jeffrey yelled.

Al Nord and Redwing arrived, and Al stepped up between us. "What's all the fuss?"

"Jeffrey found his little pajamas," Tandy said. "Everybody thought I was sissy for having a teddy bear. But Jeff wears Dumbo pajamas!"

Even Al Nord had to laugh. Redwing didn't.

"It was a mistake," Jeffrey said. "I asked Mom for Rambo pajamas, but she got Dumbo instead."

That got us chuckling even more.

"Hey, hold it," Jeffrey said. He was fumbling inside the top pocket of his Dumbo pajamas. "There's a note in here. It's from the thief!" He read the note: "EVEN SMARTBO COULDN'T CATCH ME!"

"Let me see that note," I said. Jeff handed it to me. "I don't recognize the handwriting. Does anyone else?"

The note was passed around, but no one recognized the large, printed letters.

"Gimme that note," Jeffrey said. "This is our first piece of evidence."

"Some evidence," Pinky said.

Just then Carmen walked up.

"Carmen," Tandy said. "How are you feeling?"

She tried to smile. "Look at me. What do you think?"

Carmen had pinkish stuff smeared all over her arms and legs.

"You look like the molting monsters of the planet Swump," Kaybee said.

"And that's exactly how I feel," Carmen said. "I have a fever, and Ellie Nord says I have to go home."

"Gee," Vince said. "That's too bad."

I was surprised because Vince sounded like he really meant it.

"I'm going to pack up now, but I thought I'd come down and say good-bye," Carmen said.

"Can you wait until after the archery match?" I asked. "Why don't you sit down and watch, then I'll go up and help you pack."

"Good idea," Al Nord said. "Sit over there in the shade. Let the archery competition begin!"

Redwing held up one hand for silence. He was wearing a buckskin outfit now, complete with lots of fringe that hung down at least a foot. The fringe swayed when he moved like a hundred pair of shoelaces on a clothesline.

"Before you can shoot, you must be taught the fundamentals of the legendary bow and arrow."

"What did he say?" Crunch asked Vince.

"He's gonna show us how to thwang that thang," Vince replied.

"Oh," Crunch said.

Redwing was about a hundred feet from the target. The target had three colors. Yellow on the outside ring, red on the middle ring and black for the bull's-eye circle.

"If you are right-handed," Redwing said, "the bow is held in your left hand like this. Left arm extended straight on the path you want the arrow to fly. Always aim a bit higher than your target. The farther away the target, the higher you aim. The arrow's notch goes here, and the arrow rests here. You pull back the bowstring with these two fingers. Now, watch how my ancestors wielded their prime hunting weapon.''

Redwing aimed and shot the arrow. It thunked into the target about an inch to the left of the bull's-eye.

"Wow," Dave said.

Redwing shot two more arrows and they ended up right next to each other just on the bottom edge of the bull's-eye.

"Incredible," Kaybee said.

"Now," Redwing said, "you will all get a chance to practice, then we will see whether the girls or boys are the fastest learners.''

Tandy, of course, didn't want to shoot. She sat on the grass and talked to Carmen.

Everyone took five shots, and only a few of us hit the target at all. Then we each took five more shots, and more of us hit the target. We were getting better.

"You all did very well," Redwing said. "I think you are ready to compete. Tandy, it is time that you joined us. The sides won't be even if you don't shoot. Come on, don't be afraid.''

Tandy stood. "I'm not afraid. Not at all. It's just that, well . . .''

"She's afraid of the Earth Kings!" Vince bellowed. And he and Crunch chanted, "Earth Kings! Earth Kings! Earth Kings!''

One by one, the boys each took five shots. Six arrows were in the target. Four arrows in yellow, two in red. Redwing said the yellow was five points and the red was ten points. The bull's-eye was twenty-five points, but the boys didn't hit it. Their total score was forty points.

"Girls, your turn," Redwing said.

I was first. I aimed carefully. The first arrow soared into the air and landed about ten yards past the target. I aimed lower for the second shot and sunk one into the ground. The next two missed to the left. My third arrow thunked neatly into the red.

"A red!" I yelled. "Ten points. Let's go, Blue Aliens!"

Pinky's first arrow just caught the outside edge of the yellow. All her other arrows missed by a mile.

"Five more points," she said. "That makes fifteen. Let's go Kaybee."

All of Kaybee's arrows missed.

"I am not good at flying things," she said sadly.

"We've got them beat!" Vince roared. "Earth Kings will win again!"

Tandy stepped up to the line.

"Come on, Tandy, concentrate," I said.

"But everybody's watching," she said.

"Ignore them," I said.

"We're dead," Pinky said. "The wimp won't hit a thing."

Tandy turned bright red. She whipped her head around to Pinky. "I'm not a wimp!"

Tandy snatched the bow and arrow out of Redwing's hand. With one smooth motion she notched the arrow, lifted the bow, aimed, then let loose.

Zing! Thwack!

"Ripping Rockets!" Kaybee shrieked. "An eye of the bull!"

"Bull's-eye!" I screamed.

Vince slapped his forehead. "What luck!"

Tandy shot him a hard glare. She took another arrow from Redwing, notched it, lifted the bow and . . .

Zing! Thwack!

"Another one!" Pinky exclaimed in shock.

Everybody's eyeballs were almost falling out. We couldn't believe what we were seeing.

Tandy lifted another arrow.

Zing! Thwack!

Bull's-eye.

Another one.

Zing! Thwack!

Bull's-eye. And it took a chunk out of one of her other arrows.

She notched her last arrow, aimed, then lowered it. She turned around and walked another fifty feet away. She aimed.

Ziiiing! Thwack!

A perfect bull's-eye.

Tandy handed the bow back to Redwing, whose mouth was hanging open. Then Tandy turned to Pinky.

"So, Pinky, who's the wimp now, huh?"

"How'd you *do* that?" Vince asked.

Tandy was starting to get shy again. "My father was an archery champion. We have an archery range out behind our tennis courts. He taught me how to shoot, that's all."

Dave walked up to her. "Can I have your autograph?"

We all cracked up.

"Tandy," I said, "that was absolutely terrific!"

"The Blue Aliens win!" Pinky said. "Tandy's our secret weapon! How's it feel, Earth Kings?"

"It feels lousy, okay?" Vince said.

"Yeah, but we'll get you next time," Jeffrey said. "We're still ahead of you two events to one."

"What are you talking about?" I said. "You won volleyball and the frogs. We won archery and the rope bridge."

"The rope bridge doesn't count," Dave said. "You cheated."

80

"Mr. Nord," Pinky said, "we won the rope bridge, didn't we?"

Al Nord shook his head. "Sorry, girls. That event was clearly sabotaged. You can't win by cheating, Pinky. Nope, that event doesn't count. The boys lead, two events to one."

"Yaaaaay!" The boys screamed.

"Oh, go play with your Dumbo pajamas!" Pinky yelled.

After we argued some more, the boys went off to play horseshoes for a while, and us girls helped Carmen pack up her things.

"We'll miss you, Carmen," Kaybee said.

"Thanks," Carmen said.

"You feeling okay?" Pinky asked.

Carmen shrugged. "I'll live. But I'm so itchy!"

"I had poison ivy once," Tandy said. "The more you scratch the worse it gets."

Carmen nodded. "That's what Mrs. Nord said."

"Doctor Nord," I corrected.

Pinky reached over and patted Tandy on the back. "You did great. I promise I'll never call you a wimp again."

I didn't know if Pinky was really being nice or not. Frankly, I didn't trust her. But Tandy did.

Tandy beamed. "Thanks, Pinky. I guess even I'm good for something—only I never knew it before."

"Girls," Carmen said, "you've gotta beat those guys. I hate their creepy attitude, teasing us and rubbing it in every chance they get. Make them eat their words. Try hard and win! Okay?"

"Yeah!" we all said.

"And if you find out who the sneak thief is," Carmen said, "call me right away."

"Do you have any ideas who it might be?" I asked.

"The first person I suspect is Vince," Carmen said. "I

81

think he might have stolen and hidden his own candy to take suspicion away from himself."

"Could be, could be," Pinky said. "Who else?"

"The second person I'm not really sure of," Carmen said. "And I really hope it isn't him because it's just too scary an idea."

"Who is it?" I asked.

Carmen leaned in and whispered: "Redwing."

Jeff

VINCE and Crunch rumbled off to climb some rocks, so Dave and I wandered over to play horseshoes.

"I feel like a jerk," I said. I threw a horseshoe and it missed the pit.

"I know," Dave said. "And you should. Now the whole world knows about your Dumbo pajamas."

He threw and scored a point. I decided to stop keeping track.

"Why did Mom ever buy me those!" I said between my teeth.

"The question is," Dave said, "why do you wear them?"

"Beats me," I said. "I feel like a jerk."

"Do you believe Tandy?" Dave said shaking his head. "Boy, I wish I could shoot an arrow like that."

"She really showed up Redwing. Did you see his face?"

"Yeah," Dave said, "he really hated to have a wimpy girl shoot better than he does. He's weird, isn't he?"

"Definitely."

"Think he's the sneak thief?"

I shrugged. "Maybe. Maybe not. It could be anyone."

"Even me, your best buddy?" Dave said.

"Naa," I said, not too sure.

Suddenly we heard stomping feet running our way. When I looked, I saw fat Vince and bulldozer Crunch huffing and puffing and crashing into each other as they rolled toward the horseshoe pits.

"Guys! Guys!" Vince said when they came to a halt.

"We saw them," Crunch said. "We saw the girls."

"But it's okay," Vince said, "because the Earth Kings have ruined their plan!"

"Back it up," I said. "What are you talking about?"

Vince rolled his eyes like I was stupid or something. "Down by the canoes. The girls. We saw them do it, and we really fixed their wagons!"

"Terrific," Dave said. "We're trying to win these sports competitions and you're fixing wagons for them."

"Cut the jokes," Crunch said.

The loud and long *tweeeeet* of a whistle cut through the air. "Great Treasure Hunt time!" Al Nerd yelled from the lodge.

"You can tell us later," Dave said to Crunch and Vince. "And from now on, don't fix any more wagons for those girls."

Crunch chased Dave all the way to the lodge. Vince and I walked, but I kept my distance from him. When he sweats he smells like a wet dog.

Al Nerd rounded us all up with a wave of his arms. Redwing stood beside him with a shoe box in his hand.

"The Great Treasure Hunt is about to begin," Al Nerd said. "Each of you choose a partner." We did. Dave and I chose each other. "The hunt is simple. You each get a compass and a set of directions. If you follow all the directions correctly, you will find a treasure at the end. The first team back with their treasure wins.''

Al Nerd took something from the shoe box that Redwing held. "This is a compass," Al Nerd said.

We all knew that. Then he showed us how to use it. It was easy. Then he handed each two-person team a sheet of paper with the directions.

"Any questions?" Al Nerd asked.

No one had any.

"Remember, kids, we have a peace pact."

We all mumbled that we'd try to remember.

"And," Redwing said quietly, "do nothing to disturb the Spirit of the Forest. Don't laugh. I'm serious. Mack Buster knows how serious I am. And be careful. None of these directions puts you in danger, so if you find yourself in a dangerous place, leave because you have made an error."

"This is going to be great," Dave said. "On the loose in the wilderness."

"Yup," Pinky said, "right where you belong—with the rest of the dumb animals."

"Everybody ready?" Al Nerd said. "Ready . . . set . . . go!"

We didn't go anywhere. We just stood there staring at the compass, looking at the directions on the paper, then staring back at the compass and pointing our bodies the right way. Tandy and Pinky took off to the right. Gwen and Kaybee headed left. Vince and Crunch headed farther right.

Dave read from the sheet: "Walk northeast for fifty paces until you find a pink rock."

Off we paced around the left of the lodge and into the woods. Dave was doing the counting. "Fifteen, sixteen, seventeen . . ."

It was much cooler in the shade of the woods. It smelled great in there, like fresh lawn clippings and leaves. Birds sang loudly as they zipped around high up in the sunny treetops.

"Forty-seven, forty-eight, forty-nine, fifty," Dave said. "We're here."

I looked all around us. "I don't see any pink rock. We must have made a mistake."

"Wait!" Dave said. "There it is!"

About twenty paces to our left was a large rock that was, in fact, painted pink. It must have been a trail marker or something. We went over by the rock.

"You walked crooked," I said.

"Did not," Dave said. "I was going dead northeast. The rock must have moved."

I laughed. "Yeah, that must be it. What's next?"

Dave checked the paper. "Walk northwest fifty paces, until you see a tree with no top."

"How can we see a tree with no top?" I asked.

"Let's find out," Dave said.

I took the compass and Dave looked over my shoulder. Soon we had it pointing northwest. This time I did the pacing.

"Four, five, six . . ." At thirty, I stopped. I stopped because at my feet was a stream. A wide stream. "I guess we're supposed to walk across it," I said.

"Redwing said to stay away from danger," Dave said.

"This isn't dangerous. It's just wet," I said.

Dave shrugged. "I guess. I don't see how we could have goofed. Okay, Jeff, hold your nose, here we go."

We waded across the stream. It came up to our knees, but felt good and cool.

"Forty-nine, fifty," I said. "So where's the tree with no top?"

"Where's *any* tree?" Dave said.

We stood in the center of a large, grassy clearing. The nearest tree was at least thirty paces away.

"What gives?" Dave said. "What is this, some kind of joke?"

"Come on, let's look around."

We walked all around the edge of the clearing looking for a tree with no top. We figured it would be a tree that was dead, or sawed in half, or a stump. We saw nothing like that at all.

"Somehow, Jeff, we really messed up," Dave said.

"Guess so," I said. "What do we do now?"

"Go back?" Dave asked. "Start over?"

"Do we have any choice?" I asked him.

"Yeah, we can stay here for the rest of our lives."

"Let's start over."

It took us a while, but we finally managed to find our way back to the lodge. Al Nerd spotted us and jogged over.

"Find your jellybeans already?" he said.

"Jellybeans?" Dave said. "That's the big treasure?"

"We got lost," I said. "So we're starting over."

Al Nerd took the compass. "Let me help you get started, okay What's your first direction?"

"Northeast," I said.

Al Nerd turned the compass until the needle pointed to northeast. He scratched his head, looked up at the sun, then looked back down at the compass and scratched his head again.

"No," he said. "This compass is wrong."

"Huh?" Dave said.

"There," Al Nerd said, pointing just to the side of the sun. "That's east. That's west. So northeast should be about here—almost opposite from what the compass says.

87

"I've got a feeling . . ." Dave said.

"The girls did it!" I said. "They broke the peace pact!"

Al Nerd turned bright red. "No, the girls didn't do it."

"How do you know?" Dave said.

Al Nerd smiled crookedly. "Because I guess I did it."

"What?" I said.

"Yeah, sorry," Al Nerd said. "Some of the compasses are new, some are old. The new ones were on my desk, and the old ones I was cleaning up. I remember now that when I was done cleaning them I left them on top of the Power-Vac, the huge vacuum cleaner we use. Later, I used the vacuum and forgot all about the compasses."

"So?" Dave said.

"So," Al Nerd said, "the Power-Vac is powered by a motor. The motor has large magnets inside. The motor's magnets must have reversed the magnetic field of your compass. Sorry, guys, but I'm to blame."

"Oh, great, just great," Dave said. "Here we had a good shot at beating the girls, and our compass freaks out."

"Hey, Dave," I said, "don't get so upset. There were only jellybeans out there."

"Some treasure," Dave mumbled.

"Besides," I said, "it's not fair. We all have to do the whole thing over with good compasses."

Just then, Gwen and Kaybee came yelling down the hill. "We've got it! We've found it!"

But when they saw us, they stopped running and starting looking real sad.

"We lost," Gwen said.

"The boys have been the quicker and were quicker than us," Kaybee said.

"No, no," Al Nerd said. "You were first, but—"

Then Pinky came screaming out of the woods with Tandy right behind her.

"Sabotage! Sabotage!" Pinky was hollering. She ran up to Al Nerd and held her compass in his face. "Our compass doesn't work!"

Al Nerd flexed his muscles. He took Pinky's compass. "Yup, just like Dave's and Jeff's compass. This is my fault, Pinky, I accidentally screwed up the compass. Let me see yours, Gwen." Al Nerd took her compass. "Hmmm. This is one of the new ones. This one works just fine."

"We're doing the whole thing over," Dave said to the girls.

"Now wait a minute," Pinky said to Dave. "Your compass was screwed up just like mine? So you couldn't finish?"

"That's it," Dave said.

"Then the girls win!" Pinky said.

"What are you jabbering about?" I said.

"It's simple," Gwen said. "Kaybee and I found our treasure and got back here first. You and Dave are out of it. Pinky and Tandy are out of it. Each team had a screwed up compass, so that evens things up. Kaybee and I win!"

The girls jumped around and cheered, and Dave and I just stood there knowing they were right. Until I thought of something.

"Wait, wait, wait, wait," I said. "You won *only* if Vince's and Crunch's compass is okay. If it's screwed up, we have to do the whole thing over."

"Jeff's right," Al Nerd said. "If Gwen and Kaybee are the only ones with a good compass, that isn't fair. We'll just have to wait for Crunch and Vince."

So, we waited. And waited. And waited.

"Think anything happened to them?" Tandy asked.

Redwing stepped up. "Maybe I should look for them."

"No, give them a little more time," Al Nerd said.

So, we waited.

Ten minutes later, we heard them.

"Blubber brain!" Crunch yelled.

"Walrus face!" Vince yelled back.

"Eat slime!" Crunch bellowed.

"Lick leeches!" Vince said.

They burst out of the underbrush like a couple of rhinos.

"Wow!" Dave said. "Look at them!"

"They must have been fighting," Pinky said.

They were dirty from head to foot. Pieces of leaves were stuck in their wild hair and plastered on their ripped T-shirts.

"How would you like another sock in the gut, fatso?" Crunch said.

"You think this boy is afraid of a slug like you?" Vince said. "My fists are bigger than yours!"

"Are not!"

"Are!"

They held up their fists and compared them.

By this time, we had all run up to them.

"What's going on?" Al Nerd said.

Crunch pointed to Vince. "He's a turtle."

"And you're a meatloaf," Vince said back.

"Where's your compass?" Al Nerd asked.

The two large guys looked at each other. They said together: "He broke it."

"Broke it?" Al Nerd said.

Vince shrugged. "We got fighting and we don't know how it broke. I'm sorry."

"Me, too," Crunch said. Crunch handed Al Nerd the shattered compass.

"Now," Al Nerd said, "this is very important. Did the compass work?"

We all leaned in to hear the answer. Victory or defeat hung in the balance.

"I guess it worked," Vince said, "when Crunch here didn't goof up. And, boy, did he goof!"

"Did not!" Crunch said. "Your paces were too big, and you walk crooked."

"You thought southeast was southwest!" Vince said.

"Hold it!" Al Nerd said. "Stop the fighting right now. Don't worry about the compass. Accidents will happen, I guess. Sorry, girls, it looks like we'll never know if their compass worked or not. We have to do the whole hunt over again."

"Not fair!" Tandy whined.

"Crunch," Gwen said quickly, "what were you two fighting about anyway?"

"Blubber boy started it," Crunch said.

"Oh, don't be a baby," Vince said to him. Then he said to us, "Crunch is just mad because I ate all the jellybeans."

"The *jellybeans!*" Gwen said.

"You found them?" Pinky said.

"Yeah," Crunch said.

"Then your compass must have been working!" Tandy said.

"And that means . . . that means . . ." Kaybee said.

"The girls win!" Pinky cheered.

And the girls danced and pranced like fools.

"They won?" Crunch asked.

I explained to Crunch and Vince how the girls won.

"Me and my big mouth," Vince said. "Why'd I have to tell them about the jellybeans."

"We probably would have won if we'd run right back here instead of fighting," Crunch said.

Pinky yelled, "It's all tied up, boys. The Blue Aliens

91

have won two events. And you stupid Earth Kings have won two. What's next, Mr. Nord?''

''The canoe race,'' he said.

The girls started giggling again. Then Vince and Crunch burst into laughter. Then Al Nerd started chuckling!

What the heck was so funny?

I soon found out when we all stood by the canoe docks, ready for the canoe race.

''Here's the way it's going to happen,'' Al Nerd said. ''First, you choose a partner. Then you run from this starting line to your canoes, which, as you can see, are waiting there on the shore. Then you race out to where Redwing is sitting in that rowboat, canoe around him, and the first canoe back here wins. Any questions?''

Nobody had any questions.

''Ready?'' Al Nerd called to Redwing. Redwing waved back. ''Ready, kids?''

''Yeah. Sure. Let's go,'' we all said.

''Ready. Set.'' And Al Nerd blew his whistle.

We ran for our canoes. Gwen and Kaybee got to theirs first.

''Oh, no!'' Gwen yelled.

''What is this stuff?'' Kaybee said.

''Mr. Nord! Mr. Nord!'' Pinky yelled. ''The boys greased our canoe paddles!''

''No we didn't!'' Vince said. ''We saw *you* grease *our* paddles, so we switched paddles on you. Double-whammy sabotage!''

So that's what everybody had been giggling about. The girls greased the boys' paddles. But what they didn't know was that Vince and Crunch gave them the greased paddles back.

''Hey!'' Crunch said. ''Our paddles are greased, too!''

"What?" I said. "How did we *all* end up with greasy paddles?"

Al Nerd said, "I saw everything that happened. So I made sure that *everyone* got greased paddles!"

"Wow!" Vince said. "Triple-whammy sabotage!"

"You think your sneaky tricks are funny?" Al Nerd said. "You think you can break the peace pact? Well, let's see how you race now! The race is still on! Go!" And he blew his whistle again.

So, with the paddles slipping around in our hands, we took off. Before we were even ten feet, Dave's paddle squirted from his hands and floated away.

"Paddle with your hands!" I yelled.

"Good idea!" And Dave was soon churning away at the water.

Brainy Gwen got an idea. "Use the other end, Kaybee," she said. "Turn your paddle upside down, there's no grease on the wide end."

"Mega-smart, Gwendolyn," Kaybee said.

Using the narrow end of their paddles, Gwen and Kaybee began to move out.

Crunch and Vince were in the lead. They had chucked their paddles immediately and were flapping away with their fat hands.

"Earth Kings! Earth Kings!" Vince was chanting.

Pinky and Tandy had another idea. They were using their sneakers as paddles! And they were really picking up speed, too.

As we all rounded Redwing sitting in his rowboat, we rammed into each other about fifty times, then started heading back for shore.

Vince and Crunch were pooping out.

"My hands are getting all wrinkly in this water," Vince said.

93

"Then use your face," Crunch said, wheezing.

Pinky and Tandy would have beaten Dave and me if Tandy hadn't seen a fish. She yanked her hands out of the water and screamed: "Shark!"

Their canoe slowed down immediately and Dave and I coasted quickly into shore ahead of them.

"We won!" Dave yelled.

Dave and I shook hands. "All right!" I said. "Now it's up to Crunch and Vince. If they can beat Gwen and Kaybee, we'll win the event! Go! Go!"

But Gwen and Kaybee were now ahead by about five feet.

Dave started screaming at Vince and Crunch. "Come on, you two hippos! You fat, lazy beach balls. Move those blubbery butts! Are you going to be slow-motion slobs all your lives?"

Crunch lifted his head and shot an angry glare at Dave. "Did you hear what he called us?"

"Yeah," Vince said. "Nobody talks to this boy like that!"

And they really started moving out.

"Elephants!" Dave yelled. "Blobs!"

It worked. Crunch and Vince just beat Gwen and Kaybee—mainly because Gwen was laughing so hard about what Dave called Crunch and Vince.

"The Earth Kings win!" I announced.

"The Blue Aliens just couldn't do it," Dave said, smiling. Then his smile vanished when he saw dripping-wet Vince and Crunch marching right toward him.

"Beach balls?" Crunch roared.

"Slow-motion slobs?" Vince snarled.

"Heh-heh," Dave said. "Well, I think I'll just take a little jog." And he took off, with the two wide giants right behind him.

"Great race," I said to Gwen.

She grinned. "I'll have to admit, it was a lot of fun. Good race, J.M."

Gwen offered her hand and I shook it.

"The boys lead the events three to two," Al Nerd said.

"YAAAAAAAA!" the Earth Kings screamed.

The Blue Aliens were already walking away.

When I got back to the tent, Dave was changing.

"How far did Vince and Crunch chase you?" I asked.

"Not far. They ran out of steam after a while and sat down on a log."

"What'd you do?"

"I went back and told them I didn't mean anything I said. I just wanted them to win."

"Did they believe you?" I asked.

"They threw me in the lake."

I broke up.

Soon we gathered in the cafeteria for dinner. For the first time since we'd been at camp, we all sat together at the same table. Otto and Happy had made a meal we all loved—pizza! As we munched, we laughed and laughed about everything that happened during the greasy canoe race. But our laughter suddenly stopped when Al Nerd stormed into the room.

"Stop eating!" he said. "I want to know, and I want to know *now!* Who took my whistle?"

"Oh, no," Gwen said. "The sneak thief strikes again!"

We all looked at each other. Our smiles were gone, and once again we all wondered which one of us was the sneak thief.

"I want my whistle!" Al Nerd said like a little kid. "And I want it before dark!" He cursed and left the cafeteria.

"What do you think, J.M.?" Gwen whispered.

I leaned in to her. "I don't know. Maybe one of us is sleepwalking or something."

"During the day?" she said.

"Awake-walking?" I said.

She popped her lips and shook her head. "Listen, Jeffrey, if this thief does whatever he or she has done before, that whistle is going to turn up in a weird place, right?"

"Right," I said. "So?"

"So, if we keep an eye on everybody, sooner or later one of them will try to put the whistle someplace where Al Nord will find it."

"Right," I said. "But how do we watch everybody?"

"Good point, J.M.," Gwen said. "How about if we each follow one suspect? I'll follow Pinky. And I think you should follow Vince."

"What about Crunch?" I said.

Gwen shrugged. "Or Dave. Or Redwing. Carmen thought Redwing might be the thief, but how do we follow him?"

"We can't. Listen, I'll follow Vince. He and Crunch always hang around together anyway, so I'll be following two for the price of one."

"Great," Gwen said. "We'll meet later and compare notes. Good luck."

Since my assignment was to follow Vince, I had to sit there and watch him and Crunch devour pizza.

The only trouble was that I had to go to the bathroom. I sat there as long as I could, but soon I couldn't wait any longer. I hurried off to the bathroom at the far end of the cafeteria. When I came back out, both Vince and Crunch were gone.

Gwen

"HI, Gwendolyn," Kaybee said as I came out of the cafeteria.

"Hi," I said.

Pinky was up ahead of me, walking back toward her tent. The last thing I needed was for Kaybee to be hanging around while I spied on Pinky.

"Would you like to teach me how to play the shoe horses?" Kaybee asked.

I laughed. "That's horseshoes, Kaybee. Sorry, not right now. I, um, have to go back to the tent and do some, um, things."

"Oh," Kaybee said. "Well, I'll just travel alone, then."

Kaybee sounded so sad and I really did want to keep her company, but Pinky just disappeared around the back of her tent and I had to find out what she was up to.

Then Dave came out of the trading post, just in the nick of time.

"Dave," I called.

Dave came over with a puzzled expression on his face. "What are you up to?"

"Nothing," I said. "Kaybee would like to play some horseshoes, but I've got some stuff to do. Will you play with her?"

"Okay," Dave said.

"You will?" Kaybee said.

"Sure," Dave said. "I'll show you some trick shots, too."

"Maximum!" Kaybee said. "Bye, Gwen!"

Kaybee and Dave went off toward the horseshoe pits. They sure were getting along. The prankster boy and the strange girl. What a pair.

Then I remembered my mission and ran up to the tents. When I got there, Pinky was nowhere to be seen. She wasn't in her tent, in the bath house, or anywhere up in the woods.

What now? And where was Tandy?

I decided to search for them.

I walked a wide circle up through the woods behind the tents, then I made my way down toward the activities field.

And there they were.

Off in the distance, Kaybee and Dave were throwing horseshoes. But in front of them and nearer to me were Pinky and Tandy. I had to sit down on a rock I was so shocked. They were having *fun* together! Tandy was showing Pinky how to shoot a bow and arrow on the archery range. Ellie Nord was there to watch them. It looked like friendships sure were changing.

"Boo!"

I jumped up from the rock and spun around. "Jeffrey! Don't do that!"

Jeffrey was chuckling. "Sorry, Gwen, couldn't resist. Keeping an eye on Pinky, are you? Well, what do you know—she's with Tandy."

"Amazing, isn't it?" I said. "Tandy's teaching Pinky archery. I just hope Pinky doesn't teach Tandy how to be snotty. Hey, weren't you following Vince and Crunch?"

Jeffrey looked at the ground. "I lost them. I went to the bathroom in the cafeteria, and when I came out they were gone. I have no idea where they went."

"Terrific, wonderful," I said. "Some detective you are."

"Sorry," he said.

"You might as well sit down, Jeffrey," I said. "As long as we keep an eye on those four kids down there, if any sneak thiefing goes on, we'll know Vince or Crunch did it."

"Or Redwing or Al or Ellie Nerd," Jeffrey said.

"Yeah . . . well," I said.

We sat in silence for a minute, watching the strange twosomes down below. A horseshoe clanked, and Kaybee squealed with joy. Kaybee's squealing made Pinky miss her shot.

"Listen, Gwen, something's really been bothering me."

"What?"

"I'm dying to know what really scared Mack."

"Probably his own imagination," I said.

"Yeah," Jeffrey said. "Or the Spirit of the Forest."

"Be sensible," I said. "Redwing is filling everybody's head with that legend. Sure, it's spooky. But is it real? I doubt it."

Jeffrey chuckled. "I'll tell you, Gwen, sleeping out here in the woods with ghosts stories and all that has got me jumping, too."

"Everybody's jumping," I said. "Tandy pinned her tent flaps closed last night, and Kaybee actually wants to see the ghost—she thinks she can talk it out of scaring us!"

"I hope she does," he said.

I looked down toward the archery range. "Oh, no! Where did everybody go!" Pinky, Tandy, Dave, and Kaybee had vanished. "Terrific. Here I sit jabbering while our suspects just walk away."

"Some detective you are," Jeffrey said with a big grin.

I laughed. "What time is it?"

"Seven forty-five."

"Come on, let's see what's going on."

Dusk was settling quietly over Camp Arrowhead. The sun had slipped below the treetops without anybody noticing, and now the sky was a deep gray-blue.

We were almost to the lodge when Kaybee suddenly appeared.

"Gwendolyn," she said, "have you seen the fat moon? It's really alive tonight. Look!"

We looked where she was pointing. The biggest, fattest, brightest full moon I'd ever seen was rising in the sky like a searchlight.

"Wow," Jeffrey said. "A vampire moon."

"Knock it off, Jeffrey," I said, whacking his arm.

When we walked inside the lodge, everyone was already there.

"Oh, boy. Oh, boy," Vince was saying. He was finally getting his wish. Ellie Nord had brought out some marshmallows and everyone was roasting them on sticks over the tall flames in the fireplace.

"I like mine burnt to a crisp," Vince said, almost drooling.

"Not me," Pinky said. "I like them when they get nice and runny inside."

Jeffrey and I grabbed sticks and started roasting our own.

"I have a surprise tonight, kids," Al Nord said. "Instead of a campfire, I've asked Redwing to take you all on a night walk.''

"A night walk?" Tandy asked. "What's that?"

"You know," Al Nord said, "a tour of the woods after dark. How many of you have ever been in the woods after dark?"

"Not me," Tandy said. "It sounds scary."

"I have," Kaybee said. "The clicking and hooing sounds are like music for the stars to dance by."

Crunch shook his head and rolled his eyes. "What a weirdo."

"You think fighting over jellybeans isn't weird?" Dave asked.

Crunch glared at him. "Ever try talking with a fist in your mouth?"

"Now, *that's* weird," Dave said.

"So," Al Nord continued, "as soon as we're done with the marshmallows, it should be dark enough to begin."

When most of the marshmallows were in Vince's stomach, we wandered outside to the back patio of the lodge, where Redwing was waiting for us.

"I have bad news," Redwing said, shaking his head.

"Bad news?" Al Nord asked.

"Yes," Redwing said. "The Spirit of the Forest is restless tonight. I am not sure it is safe to walk in the woods."

Crunch elbowed Vince and whispered, "He's scared."

"There have been signs," Redwing said. "Always when darkness falls, the night breezes blow and the lake ripples in the moonlight. This is how my ancestors traveled at night—the breeze hid their scent and brought them the scents of dangerous night animals, and the ripples on the lake helped them locate the shoreline and jutting rocks.

101

But tonight, there is no breeze. The lake is still. This is *not* a good sign.''

I took a long look around the lake. The sharp yellowish moonlight was illuminating the lake and casting the black shadows of trees far over the glasslike water. I had to admit, it did look eerie out there.

"But the moonlight helps you see, doesn't it?" Al Nord asked.

Redwing nodded. "Also, it helps other things see *us*. No, the spirit is out tonight. This is no night for humans.''

I couldn't figure Redwing out. I was certain he was lying. But why?

Al Nord shrugged. "Sorry, kids. If Redwing says it is too dangerous, then I guess it is. Anybody for some more marshmallows?''

"This boy is!" Vince said loudly.

Redwing left, and we were all mumbling when we went back into the lodge. Vince raced right for a half a bag of marshmallows, snatched it off a table, and flopped down in front of the fire.

"Hey, Mr. Nord!" Vince called.

"Yes?''

"Guess what?''

"What, Vince?''

"I found your whistle!''

"What?''

Vince held up the marshmallow bag. "It was in here with the marshmallows. And there's a note.''

"A note?" Al Nord took his whistle and the note from Vince. He read the note aloud. The note contained only one word: "Gotcha!''

"The Spirit of the Forest strikes again." Dave chuckled.

Al Nord scanned the room and all our faces. "One of

you snuck back in here when we were talking with Redwing. Who did it?''

No one confessed.

"Ellie, did you see anyone?'' Al asked.

"Nope. I was in the other room.'' She smiled. I think Ellie found all of this kind of funny. I liked her.

"I hate these gags,'' he said. "If my whistle is broken, there's going to big trouble.''

We all began to chatter about the mysterious whistle theft and all the other strange happenings.

Then Ellie Nord started us all singing for the next hour or so. Fat Vince said he could shatter a glass with his voice. He didn't, of course, but out in the woods somewhere a dog started howling.

Just before ten o'clock, we all headed for our tents. I paused and gazed back over the lodge and the lake. The night was crystal clear and the moon was so bright it glinted off the canoe bottoms down at the dock. Way up on the other side of the lake I could see Redwing's campfire winking through the trees.

"It's everything!'' Kaybee said to me.

"Huh?''

"Remember, Gwendolyn, at the first campfire sing I said day and night were different because each showed different things?''

"Yes, I remember,'' I said. "You said the day shows the earth and the night shows the sky. You said it was a brillant arrangement.''

"Yes!'' Kaybee said. "But now, this night, with the spotlight moon, it is everything. It is both day and night together. All the stars are looking down and seeing the earth. Look, I have a shadow!''

"Hey!'' Dave said, coming up to us. "That's *my* shadow! You stole it! You must be the sneak thief!''

103

"Oh, David!" Kaybee said, laughing. "This can't be your shadow. Your shadow would never fit me!"

Dave laughed. "Yeah, it would be all baggy."

Kaybee and Dave chuckled together, then we finally said good night and went back to our tents.

Twenty minutes later, the whole camp was dead silent, like it was waiting for something, like the trees and rocks were listening hard into the night. Cuddling up in my cot, only a little frightened, I soon started drifting off into a nice, easy sleep.

"Oooooooooo-unga!"

My eyes flew open.

"What was that?" Kaybee whispered.

"I don't know," I said. "Maybe it's that dog we heard before."

"Waaaahhhhhhh-mootoo!"

"I think it is no doggy," Kaybee said.

"Nope," I said, swallowing, "definitely no dog."

"WOOO-WOOOOOOOOOO-RRRAARR!"

Tandy shrieked from the tent next door, "It's the Spirit of the Forest!"

Kaybee and I sat up in our cots. Neither of us moved a muscle. We just stared at each other, our heads cocked and listening hard.

No more sounds came.

"Maybe the boys are pulling a gag," I whispered.

"Maybe a gag is pulling them," Kaybee said.

"Let's go back to sleep," I said.

"WAH-WAH-WAH-WAH-WHOOO!"

"Screaming scampies!" Kaybee said. "Indian dancing sounds!"

Suddenly we heard the bushes rustle behind our tent. Then heavy footsteps shuffled through the leaves and loose

104

rocks. Then the footsteps grew louder until they stopped right outside our tent.

"Gwen? Kaybee?" Vince whispered.

I opened our tent flap and Vince shined a flashlight in my eyes. "Get that out of my face. What are you guys doing out there?"

"Did you hear that noise?" Crunch asked.

"Yes," I said. "What on earth was it?"

"Maybe it was *nothing* on earth," Kaybee said.

Jeff and Dave appeared behind Crunch and Vince. The moonlight turned their hair to orange-yellow.

"I'll be honest with everybody," Dave said. "I'm scared out of my brain."

Pinky and Tandy arrived, too, and Kaybee and I went outside to join the group of frightened kids.

Pinky said, "Did you hear the—"

"*Ooooooooo-waaaaaaaa—tumba!*"

My back prickled and I noticed my eyes were drying out from bulging so much.

"What *is* it?" Crunch asked.

"Where's it coming from?" Jeffrey asked.

"Redwing was right," Tandy said. "There *is* a ghost out here."

Nobody told Tandy she was wrong.

"*Wooooooooooooo.*"

Pinky pointed down toward the lodge. "There. It came from down there, I'm sure it did."

When I looked, I saw something dark slip into the shadows.

"Did you see that?" Dave whispered.

"Who was it?" Kaybee asked.

"*What* was it?" Vince said.

"Vince, shine your flashlight down there, quick," I said.

Just when Vince raised his flashlight, it went out. "Darn," he said. He shook it and banged it against his thigh. It still wouldn't light.

"Terrific, just terrific," Jeffrey said.

"*WOO—WOO—STAY AWAY—FROM THE—FORRRR-REST!*"

Tandy shrieked: "T-the Sp-spirit of the F-forest!"

"There!" Jeffrey said. His finger shook as he pointed to blackness down between the lodge and the boat dock. "I saw someone down there."

All of us saw a shadowy figure zip into the darkness. And before anyone could speak it suddenly moved out of the shadows and into a shaft of golden moonlight. It paused briefly there, then disappeared once again into the deep shadows of the woods.

"Hopping hippos!" Kaybee said. "It was *Redwing!*"

We were too stunned to say anything for about a full minute.

Then Vince said, "I've got it! Redwing is trying to scare us!"

We all looked at Vince, and all together said: "*No kidding!*"

"The point is," I said, "why?"

"No, Gwen," Pinky said, "the point is: What are we going to do about it?"

"Good point," Jeffrey said.

"Listen," Pinky said, "I'm not going to sit around and let Redwing get away with this. I say let's get back at him."

"How?" Vince asked.

"Redwing was heading back toward his camp," Pinky said. "Let's go down there, right now, and scare the pants off him."

"Well, what are we waiting for?" Dave said.

106

"Come on," Vince said, "follow me!"

Fat Vince ended up following us because we all ran fast toward the woods and Redwing's teepee. The moonlight lit our way as we rushed silently down the path that hugged the shoreline of Lake Hoppipong. Frogs and other night creatures croaked and buzzed as we passed them. Soon, Redwing's teepee came into sight. A light blue light was seeping out from his tent flaps.

"He's watching his TV," Jeffrey whispered.

"What now?" Tandy asked.

Pinky had a plan and she told us all about it. We split up into twos and spread out around Redwing's teepee, then moved in close. Pinky waved to me, I waved back. We were ready.

"Oooooooooo," Pinky ooed.

"What?" we heard Redwing say.

"Arrrooooooo!" Dave howled like a wolf or something. Redwing turned down the sound on his TV.

Dave was laughing so much he had to clamp a hand over his mouth.

Pinky signaled again and we all placed our hands on his teepee. We began to shake it.

Pinky nodded to Crunch and Crunch nodded back.

"Boooooo," Crunch said. Pinky rolled her eyes. Crunch continued. "Booo! You have made the Spirit of the Forest angry!"

We shook the teepee harder. We heard Redwing scuffling about. Dave was now giggling so hard he had to run a few steps away.

"Boooo-woooo!" Crunch said. "You have made *fun* of the Spirit! I do not *like* that. In fact, I think it *stinks!* Prepare to *DIE!*"

We shook the teepee furiously, all the while making wooing and growling sounds.

"No!" Redwing shouted.

I nodded to Pinky and Pinky nodded to everyone else.

We stopped shaking the teepee. Then we all moved around to the entrance of Redwing's teepee.

"Are you still out there?" Redwing asked. Slowly, Redwing parted the flaps of the teepee. He carefully stuck out his head.

"BOOO!" we all screamed.

Redwing yelped and fell back on his butt inside his teepee. We all stormed inside.

"The kids!" Redwing screeched.

"What do you mean trying to scare us, you creep!" Crunch roared.

"Yeah!" Jeffrey said. "Spirit of the Forest—*ha!*"

"I didn't do it!" Redwing pleaded. "I *didn't!*"

Kaybee stood over him and shook her head. "Just like the Lizard Liars of the planet Forked-Tongue."

"Why'd you do it?" Vince asked. "Come on, *talk!*"

Redwing's shoulders slumped. "I can't understand it. It worked with all the other kids we've had at camp."

"What worked?" I demanded.

Redwing sighed. "Whenever kids start to cut up and make trouble, Al tells me to give them the Spirit of the Forest story to scare them into behaving. But you kids are different. It didn't work."

"Al Nord is behind this?" I said. I couldn't *believe* it.

"A conspiracy!" Jeffrey said. "Yeah, Redwing, we're onto you now. It's all over, fella. Might as well spill all the beans."

Jeffrey looked at me all cocky-like. I closed my eyes and shook my head. What a silly kid.

"I don't know what you're talking about," Redwing said.

"Then I'll tell you," Dave said. "You're the sneak thief, aren't you?"

"No!" Redwing yipped. "Believe me, I'm not. I only tried to scare you so you wouldn't get into trouble. Like the Cursed Cave. There's no such thing. But if I didn't say there was, you might have gone inside and gotten hurt. I was only trying to protect you."

"Gee, you mean there's no treasure in the cave?" Vince said.

"No," Redwing said. "And I'll tell you the whole truth. I tied your clothes together too. That was Al's idea to quiet you guys down, to make you think the Spirit of the Forest did it."

"I think we ought to have a talk with big Al Nerd," Vince said.

Before we could do anything, Al Nord himself came into the tent. "I heard screaming up here. What's going on?" He took a look at our faces. "Uh-oh."

"We know what you've been up to," I said angrily. "And we don't like it one bit. After all your lectures about no more sneaky tricks, *you've* been behind them all along. Frankly, Mr. Nord, I find that detestable."

"Yeah," Jeffrey said. "You even scared Mack away!"

Redwing's eyes flew wide. "We didn't scare Mack away. Perhaps he was frightened by my stories, but he said he saw a ghost. I wasn't a ghost until tonight."

"Poo-bah, I do not believe that," Kaybee said. "You must have done it."

"Let's throw him in the lake!" Crunch hollered.

"Hold it, hold it!" Al Nord said. "First of all, Mack probably scared himself. Second of all, I was wrong and Redwing was wrong. I'm sorry. Redwing is sorry, too. Third of all, how are you going to throw me into the lake when I've got these?" He flexed his muscles a few times.

"Ha!" Vince laughed. "This big boy has seven other

friends right here who can handle those muscles of yours. Why, I'll bet I could carry you all by myself!''

"Hold it," Al Nord said. "Okay, you win. Look, you've been pulling pranks and Redwing and I have been pulling pranks. We're even.''

"Maybe," I said. "How do we know you're not the sneak thief?''

"Now wait just a minute!" Al Nord said. "I'm no thief. I was with most of you when all those things were taken.''

"Then it's Redwing!" Jeff shouted.

"No, it's not Redwing," Al Nord said. "It's one of *you*. Now, come on, sit down, let's talk. I have an idea.''

We all sat Indian-style on the carpeted floor of Redwing's teepee.

"Now," Al Nord said. "Let's have some fun for a change. Let's plan something for tomorrow that's going to be a blast.''

"Like what?" Tandy asked.

"A Great Showdown," Al Nord said. "Boys against girls. Blue Aliens against Earth Queens.''

"Earth *Kings*," Vince said.

We all laughed.

"Right," Al Nord said. "It will be a once-and-for-all, sabotage-proof sports and activities showdown. And the winning team gets to throw both me and Redwing in the lake.''

"With all your clothes on," Vince added.

"All right," Al Nord said, "with all our clothes on.'' Redwing shook his head.

"Sounds perfect," Pinky said. "Tell us how the showdown works.''

"Nope," Al Nord said. "That's what makes it sabotage-proof. No one but me and Redwing will know what the

110

events will be until tomorrow. The boys lead three to two. They won volleyball, the frog race, and the canoe race. The girls won archery and the compass treasure hunt. We'll add the scores of the Great Showdown events to that, and this time it will be fair and square. What do you say?''

"I say it sounds like fun," I said. "But first, you and Redwing have to promise not to scare us anymore—or scare any more kids at camp. What if we were so scared we ran off into the woods? Or ran after Redwing and fell into the lake?"

Al Nord nodded. "You're right, of course. It's just that you guys have been such troublemakers we really didn't know what to do. But we promise."

"Thank you," I said.

"And now," Redwing said, "because I feel so bad about this whole thing, I have a present for each of you. I have been digging around this camp for a couple of years now. I have found many things, including flint arrowheads. I would like you each to have one."

Out of his leather pouch Redwing took eight authentic Indian flint arrowheads and gave us each one.

"Gee!" Dave said. "Thanks!"

"This is great," Crunch said.

I studied my arrowhead very closely, running my fingertips over the old artifact and fantasizing about the great warriors of the past.

On the way back to our tents, all of us were yapping about the Great Showdown tomorrow.

"It sounds like it will be mega-hard," Kaybee said.

"Don't worry," I said. "You'll at least do as well as Vince."

"Are you talking about Superboy?" Vince said, smiling wide.

111

"No, we're talking about Blubberboy," Pinky said.

"I don't know about the rest of you," Jeffrey said, "but I feel great. We cracked the case of the Spirit of the Forest. We'd make a great detective team, wouldn't we?"

"Eight detectives?" I said, laughing.

"No, not eight detectives," Tandy said. "*Seven* detectives—and *one* sneak thief."

That really wiped the smiles off our faces.

"Looks like we still have a mystery to solve," Jeff said to me.

"Yes, J.M., it certainly does. And time is running out."

"But," Jeffrey said. "I have an idea. A great idea."

"Oh, no. Everytime you get an idea, Jeffrey, it turns into trouble."

"And this time, Gwen, I have a *great* idea! But I can't tell you until I'm sure *you're* not the sneak thief."

"Jeffrey!"

"Sleep tight!"

Even though I was mad at Jeffrey for thinking I was the sneak thief, and even though I was still angry over what Redwing and Al Nord had been doing, I slept like a baby. My last thought before drifting off to sleep was that even if we don't catch the sneak thief, we'll have terrific fun tomorrow at the Great Showdown.

And I was right.

And I was wrong.

Jeff

"**S**HAKE IT UP, BABY!"

My eyes flew open and I sat up in my cot.

"TWIST AND SHOUT!"

I wriggled a finger in my ear. Was I really hearing The Beatles? Where was I? Yeah, in my tent at camp. The music rocked on. What time was it? I checked my watch. Seven o'clock in the morning.

"Great! Great!" Dave said. I looked over and he was flip-flopping around on his cot and laughing his redheaded head off.

The Beatles' driving beat was still blasting all over camp.

"What gives?" I said.

"Great, isn't it?" Dave said. "Instead of a bugle waking us up, we get The Beatles!"

I started to giggle. "Did you do this?"

Dave nodded about fifty times. "Last night, after we left Redwing's teepee, Al Nerd asked me to put on the reveille record this morning. When I went down there the record player that hooked up to the loudspeaker was ready to go, and the bugle record was already on. But I saw another stack of records sitting there, so I put one on!''

Suddenly the rock music stopped with a loud screech. Then Al Nerd's voice came over the loudspeaker.

''I KNOW WHO DID THIS—DAVE. VERY FUNNY, VERY FUNNY.''

Dave and I had a really good laugh.

The sky today was kind of silvery blue. Already the sun was beating down hard. It was going to be a hot day.

When we went down for exercises, everybody was there. But they weren't exercising. They were all gathered around Crunch McFink.

''*Little Orphan Annie???*'' Pinky said, and she bent over at the waist, laughing so much her face looked like it might explode.

''Not funny!'' Crunch said.

''What's going on?'' I asked Gwen.

''The sneak thief has struck again!'' Gwen said. ''Somebody stole Crunch's comic book—his Little Orphan Annie comic books.''

''Crunch reads Little Orphan Annie comic books?''

Fat Vince put a hand on Crunch's shoulder. ''Buddy, you'll never catch this tough boy reading Little Orphan Annie comic books.''

''Knock it off, Turtle,'' Crunch said. ''I want the crook! Ooo, I can't *wait* to get the crook!''

''I'll bet it turns up somewhere,'' Gwen said to me. ''Just like the other things.''

''I'll bet you're right,'' I said.

Crunch ranted for a while, and I kind of felt sorry for him. It seemed like all our embarrassing secrets were coming out for everybody to laugh at.

After exercises, showers, breakfast, and outdoor Sunday worship on a huge rock for the kids who wanted to go, we

114

all met Al Nerd and Redwing in the woods for an Artifact Hunt.

"So when's the Great Showdown?" Dave asked.

Al Nerd laughed. "I'll tell you all about it later. We'll meet after lunch to prepare. For now, take it away, Redwing." Al Nerd left.

"First," Redwing said, "I am really sorry about last night. I acted stupidly. My ancestors who inhabited these woods would be ashamed of me. Still, I inherited their love of nature. Come on, let me show you their land."

First he took us on a long walk through the woods to a high ridge. From up there you could see the whole valley, all the way to the shopping mall in the distance.

"Wow!" Kaybee said. "This is more of the planet than I have ever seen all at once."

"I wouldn't mind living out here," Dave said.

"Be serious," I said.

"I am," Dave said. "I've always liked this stuff—camping out, lots of trees, sneaking around and exploring. See that light spot in the rock there?"

"Yup," I said.

"Pink quartz. See that glittery, flaky stuff in that rock? Mica. And I'll bet you don't know what kind of tree that is. I'll tell you. White ash. And there's a sugar maple. You'll find those trees mostly in the eastern woodlands."

I could only stare at my nutty friend. I never knew he knew so much about this stuff. I suddenly felt kind of dumb.

"Look up, David," Kaybee said. "A lovely cumulus cloud."

"Is that what that is?" Dave said. "It looks like a car."

"It does!" Kaybee said. "And there's a mouse!"

Kaybee and Dave wandered off, pointing out this and that and giggling to each other.

115

"So what do you think, Crunch?" wide Vince said as he looked over the valley. "Great, huh? Makes you feel big, doesn't it?"

"Yeah," Crunch said. "Makes me wanna fly right over the trees."

"Need any help?" Pinky said, laughing.

"So, Jeffrey," Gwen said, "what's the big plan for catching the sneak thief? Am I a suspect?"

"No, you're not a suspect," I said. "And I can't tell you my plan until later."

"You mean until you have one."

"Something like that," I said.

Redwing led us back down the path through woods until we came to the artifact area he showed us on the first day of camp.

"Now," Redwing said, "we are going to explore the earth for evidence of my Indian ancestors."

For the next half hour, we dug around the area. I found a piece of pottery. All of us found neat things to take home.

"Slipping snakelings!" Kaybee said. "What's this?"

We all gathered around Kaybee. There, stuck into the ground, was a stick. Stuck on the stick was a piece of paper. I plucked it off and read the words: "HERE LIES LITTLE ORPHAN ANNIE. GOT YOU AGAIN!"

"The thief!" Tandy said.

We dug into the ground and, sure enough, there was Crunch's comic book.

"It's all dirty!" Crunch said. "Wait till I get that crook."

I took a quick look around for evidence. And just when Redwing said it was time to go back, I found something.

It was lying at the base of a tree near where Kaybee

found the buried comic book. It was an arrowhead like the ones that Redwing had given us last night.

So, while the rest of the kids went off canoeing and swimming, Gwen and I headed off to do some figuring.

"So, what do you figure?" I asked.

"I don't know. What do you figure?"

"I don't know."

We weren't getting anywhere, except farther up the path into the woods. Soon we came to the gurgling stream that ran down from the hills, past Redwing's teepee, past the campfire area, and right to where we happened to be right then.

"Let me see that arrowhead you found again," Gwen asked.

I gave it to her. She studied it. "This is the key to the plan to catch the sneak thief."

"I already know that," I said. "The thief dropped this when he or she buried Crunch's comic book. All we have to do is find out who dropped it."

"How?" she asked.

Boy, I hated it when she put me on the spot like that. "Okay, smarty, you tell me."

Gwen smiled. "It's simple. We go to each kid, ask to see his or her arrowhead, and the kid without one is the sneak thief."

"Right!" I said. "What are we waiting for?"

It sure was great to have a brainy friend.

When we got back to the lodge, all the other kids were changing out of their bathing suits. Soon, we were all in the cafeteria for lunch. I started asking questions.

"Hey, Pinky," I said, "how about you showing me the arrowhead Redwing gave you."

"Why should I?" she said.

117

"If you don't have yours, you're the thief, that's why,"
I said.

"Go jump in the lake," she said. "And quit calling me
a thief!"

Gwen dragged me away by the arm. "Terrific, J.M.
Nobody's going to show you anything if you call them a
thief first. Use some tact, Jeffrey. Be nice. Be sly."

"Yeah, yeah," I said. I sauntered up to where Crunch
and Vince were sucking down some apple pie.

"Hi, guys. What's going on?"

"What's it look like?" Crunch said. "We're eating."

"Yup, you sure are," I said. "Hey, those arrowheads
Redwing gave us are really neat, aren't they?"

Vince nodded. "And I've got a good one, too."

"Can I see it?" I asked.

Vince lifted his head. "No, sir."

"Oh, come on," I said, smiling wide. "I just want to
see how your arrowhead is different from mine."

Vince wiped his mouth on his sleeve. "I'm not trading,
if that's what you are thinking. No, sir."

"That's not it," I said. "Actually, see, I've got this
plan to catch the sneak thief, and—"

"And you suspect us?" Crunch growled. "Beat it before I get mad."

I shrugged and walked back to Gwen.

"Nice going, J.M.," she said.

"I tried."

I got some lunch and ate slowly, trying to think of
another way to see the arrowheads. I didn't think of
anything.

At one o'clock, Al Nerd came in.

"The Great Showdown begins in one hour," he
announced.

"YAAAY!" we all said.

118

I could feel the excitement in the room growing.

"The Earth Kings will reign!" big Vince bellowed.

"Rain?" Pinky said. "The Blue Aliens are a hurricane!" All the girls cheered.

Al Nerd held his hands up for quiet. "All of you have one hour. Be sure to change into bathing suits, T-shirts, and sneakers. Meet me down here at one, and we'll begin."

We all came out of the lodge threatening one another and laughing and getting ready to do war, then we went to our tents to change.

An hour later, we burst out of the tents and thundered down to the lodge chanting: "EARTH KINGS! EARTH KINGS! EARTH KINGS!"

We hung around down there for about five minutes, jogging in place and pretend-boxing with each other.

"BLUE ALIENS! BLUE ALIENS! BLUE ALIENS!" The girls came screaming down to the lodge.

"This is gonna be great!" Pinky said.

"Yeah, for *us!*" Vince said.

"Gee-mees," Kaybee said. "The excitement is rising high!"

Ellie Nerd came out dressed in a white tennis outfit. In her hand was a first-aid kit. Then Al Nerd came out flexing his muscles. Around his neck were two whistles and a stopwatch. In his hand was a clipboard. It was sunny, hot, we were all ready to go, and the time had finally come.

"Time for the Great Showdown," Al Nerd said.

"YAAAAAY!"

"Are you all ready?"

"YEAH!"

"Who's going to win?"

"WE ARE!"

"Are you going to play fair?"

Silence.

"Are you going to play fair, I said?"

"Yeah. Sure. Okay. If we have to," we all mumbled.

"Okay," Al Nerd said. "I want both sides to shake hands."

We all shook hands then went back to our teams.

"Okay," Al Nerd said, waving his clipboard. "I've got everything right here. Plus, I've got a few tricks worked out. Here's the setup. There are three events in water and three events on land. So everybody over to the boat dock!"

Screaming and yelling, we all ran over to the boat dock. Redwing was setting the second of two rowboats into the water. Then he hopped in a canoe, paddled out about sixty feet, and stopped there.

"Two kids on each team will do this event," Al Nerd said. "The other two kids will do the next event. The third event is a one-person event, and we'll choose who will do that out of a hat. Any questions so far?"

There were no questions.

"Okay. This is the Rowboat Sink competition. When I say go, two kids from each team hop in a rowboat and row out to where Redwing is sitting in his canoe. Inside the rowboats you will find two pots. When you get out to Redwing, take the pots and bail water *into* your rowboat until it sinks. When it sinks, swim back. The first team back on shore wins."

"Wild!" Pinky said.

"Okay, choose your sides," Al Nerd said.

Us guys immediately went into a huddle.

"We need fast rowers and swimmers," Dave said. "I think Jeff and I should go."

"Good idea," Crunch said.

"Hold it," I said. "I don't think so. Filling the boat with water will be the longest and hardest thing. If two heavy guys were in that rowboat it would be lower in the water—and *easier* to sink. I think Crunch and Vince should go.''

Vince slapped my shoulder. ''This boy has to hand it to you, Jeffrey. Brilliant thinking, brilliant.''

Crunch winked at me. ''Got it. Let's get 'em!''

We all stacked our hands together in the middle of our huddle and shouted: ''EARTH KINGS! EARTH KINGS! EARTH KINGS! YAAAAAY!''

''BLUUUUUUUUUUUUUE ALIENS!'' the girls yelled.

We were ready. Al Nerd pointed out the starting line. Crunch and Vince were ready to run to the canoe. They'd be competing against Pinky and Tandy.

''All set?'' Al Nerd said.

''Ready,'' said Crunch, Vince, Pinky, and Tandy in turn.

''Here we go,'' Al Nerd said. ''Ready . . . set . . . GO!''

Vince slipped and fell down. Kaybee thought that was really funny.

Pinky and Tandy leaped and hopped and were soon off in their rowboat, with Pinky rowing. By the time Vince and Crunch were inside their rowboat, the girls were ahead by about five yards.

''Go! Go! Go!'' everybody yelled.

The girls reached Redwing's canoe first. They brought in their oars and bent to pick up their pots.

''Hey!'' Pinky screamed. ''These aren't pots! They're frying pans! This will take forever!''

''Frying pans?'' Crunch said.

Al Nerd was chuckling hard. ''Told you there would be tricks! Better get moving!''

The girls started bailing water into their rowboat.

121

Crunch and Vince soon glided up to Redwing and began sloshing water, too.

My plan turned out to be a perfect one. With those two big guys in the rowboat, the top of the boat was only about three inches above the water and they had little trouble just scooping the water up and in, up and in. When they were done, they were so far ahead of Pinky and Tandy that the two whales floated in to shore on their backs.

"The Earth Kings are victorious!" Vince yelled.

Soon, Pinky and Tandy swam in and the other girls tried to cheer them up. "We'll get them at the next event."

Let's see," Al Nerd said. "The boys are ahead four to two."

"YAAAAAY!" we cheered.

"This stinks," Pinky said, being a really bad loser.

"What's the matter, Pinky," Dave said. "Don't you like playing fair?"

"Oooo!" Pinky said.

"Next event—to the swimming piers!" Al Nerd said.

We all hustled down the shoreline. Al Nerd stopped us under a huge tree. Hanging from a large limb of this tree was a thick rope with a loop at the bottom.

"Now, the last two kids on each side will be in the Rope Swing competition," Al Nerd said. "Listen carefully. Gwen and Kaybee, I'll use you as examples. Gwen stands on that rock, sticks her foot in the rope loop, swings out as far as she can, and jumps into the water. Kaybee stands on shore with this beach ball. When Gwen is in the water, Kaybee throws the ball to her. Gwen gets the ball, swims in, and tags Kaybee. Kaybee runs to the rock, swings out, catches the ball from Gwen, swims in, tags Gwen. You do this once more. I'll be timing this event on the stopwatch, and the best time wins. Any questions?"

"Yes," Gwen said. "How do we get the rope if it's just hanging there over the water?"

"Redwing has a long stick and he'll hand the rope to you," Al Nerd said. "All ready? It's Gwen and Kaybee against Jeff and Dave. I'll flip a coin to see which side goes first. Gwen, call it."

"Heads," Gwen said.

Al Nerd flipped the coin, caught it, then slapped it on the back of his other hand. "Heads it is. Do you want to go first or last?"

"First," Gwen said. "Ready, Kaybee?"

"We will find out," Kaybee said. She was scared.

Gwen climbed the rock and Redwing handed her the rope swing. Kaybee got the beach ball from Al Nerd.

"Ready . . . set . . . GO!" Al Nerd said, clicking his stopwatch.

Gwen swung out over the water, let go of the rope, and with her legs and arms flailing around like crazy, splashed into the water. Kaybee threw the ball. When Gwen came up to the surface it bopped her on the head. It took her a few seconds to find it, but she finally did and swam in to shore and tagged Kaybee.

Kaybee swung out on the rope screaming: "Flapping Flipdogs!" She crashed into the water. Gwen threw the ball perfectly. Kaybee swam in and tagged Gwen.

"That was mega-high flying!" Kaybee said.

The girls did it one more time around, and when Kaybee swam in to shore for the last time and tagged Gwen, Al Nerd shut off his stopwatch.

"Two minutes and sixteen seconds!" Al Nerd said.

"YAAAAY!" the girls yelled.

"Well, Dave, here we go," I said.

"Jeff, did I ever tell you I'm allergic to water?"

I laughed. "Knock it off, creep. Let's be serious!"

123

I climbed up on the rock and Redwing handed me the rope. The water looked about five miles below me and the rope felt like it was three feet thick. I stuck my foot in the loop, trying to remember to take it out when I got over the water. I was scared to death.

"Ready?" Al Nerd said.

I nodded. Dave nodded.

"Ready . . . set . . . go!"

"WHAAAAAAAAAOOOOOOO!" I said as I swung out over the water. I yanked out my foot, let go with my hands, and knew I was going to die.

The next thing I knew I was underwater. I swam up to the surface and broke into the hot air with a huge gasp. I'd made it. I'd actually done it. And it was fun! I looked over to Dave.

"Throw the ball, dummy!" I yelled.

Dave threw the ball—way, way over my head and to the left. I swam hard and finally got it, then swam like crazy to shore and tagged Dave.

I had a feeling we were already behind the girls' time, and after Dave took his swing, caught his foot, hung upside down for a second and dropped headfirst into the water, I knew we were doomed.

Still, we raced on as hard as we could. Then, at last, we were done.

"Two minutes and fifty-seven seconds. The girls win!" Al Nerd said. "No it's four to three. The boys are still ahead."

The girls cheered and jumped around for a solid minute.

"The Blue Aliens are best!" Tandy yelled.

"Not yet!" Crunch hollered.

"The next event," Al Nerd announced, "is a canoe race. One kid from each side alone in a canoe, just like the Indians used to do it. I'll choose the names out of this bag."

From his pocket, Al Nerd took a plastic bag filled with squares of paper. He reached in, plucked out two, then read the names of the kids who would compete against each other in the canoe race.

"Crunch McFink," Al Nerd said, "against Kaybee Keeper."

Pinky slapped her forehead. "We're dead," she said.

"Shut up, Pinky," Gwen said. "She'll do her best, won't you Kaybee."

"I'll try toughly," Kaybee said.

"Oh, boy. Oh, boy," fat Vince said, rubbing his hands together. "We've really got them at this one, Crunch. Go get her, boy!"

"Yeah, yeah," Crunch said.

"Nice easy strokes," I said.

"Yeah, yeah."

"You nervous?" Vince asked him.

"Yeah, yeah!"

"Crunch, Kaybee," Al Nerd said, "follow me to the canoe dock. You'll be racing from there to here at the swimming piers."

Both sides cheered on our heroes as they went with Al Nerd. Soon Crunch and Kaybee were out in the water in their canoes, ready to start the great race.

Dave turned to me. "Ever try to race a canoe by yourself?"

"No," I said.

Dave laughed. "It's hard. I mean, *very* hard. You'll see."

A minute later, we heard Al Nerd shout "Go!" and Crunch and Kaybee started paddling.

Kaybee veered off to the left and Crunch angled off to the right. Both of them were going in circles.

"Paddle on both sides!" Gwen yelled to Kaybee. "*Both* sides!"

Kaybee continued way out into the lake and Crunch circled around to meet her. They missed each other by a fraction of an inch, and went on circling. Our cheers and yells from shore soon turned into giggles and laughter as the two canoe racers did their winding dance out in the middle of the lake.

Suddenly Kaybee stood up in her canoe.

"Sit down! Sit down!" all the girls started yelling.

Kaybee smiled and waved at them. Then she walked carefully to the very rear of the canoe and sat down again. The front of her canoe lifted out of the water a little. One stroke on the left side, one stroke on the right side, and Kaybee was going straight!

"All right! All right, Kaybee!" the girls yelled.

"Look at Kaybee!" I yelled to Crunch.

Crunch looked at Kaybee. Finally he caught on and started to move toward the back of his canoe.

Meanwhile, Kaybee was picking up speed, gliding straight as an arrow right toward the swimming docks.

Crunch reached the back of his canoe, but sat down too hard. The rear of the canoe disappeared under the water and Crunch sank with it.

Kaybee crossed the finish line and won the race.

The girls went nuts.

"It's tied! It's tied!" Tandy yelled.

When Kaybee came ashore, the girls swarmed around her.

"How'd you think to go to the back of the canoe?" Gwen asked her.

"It was an experiment, that's all," Kaybee said.

When Crunch crawled out of the water, we didn't say anything to him. He was fuming mad and kicked dirt for a while, growling: "I'll get those girls. I'll get those girls. Stupid canoe. Stupid canoe."

"Everybody to the campfire area for the start of the three land events!" Al Nerd called. "It's all tied up, four to four. These events will decide which team is the Great Camp Arrowhead Champion!"

The Blue Aliens and the Earth Kings didn't walk together to the campfire area.

"Everybody ready for the three land events?" Al Nerd asked.

"YEAH!"

"The first event is the climb-and-signal competition. I'll time each team on my stopwatch, the fastest team wins. Here's how it works. Let's say the girls start first. When I say go, one girl climbs this tree right here. The second girl climbs that tree way over there. I'll hand the first girl a secret message she has to relay to the second girl—without speaking. When the second girl thinks she knows the message, she writes it down and runs back here and hands it to me. It's something like the Indians used to do, and you have to use your imagination. Any questions?"

"Sounds impossible," Crunch said.

"Not for us brilliant girls!" Gwen said.

"We'll win," Dave said. "The girls can't communicate without talking all the time."

Al Nerd flipped a coin and the girls won. They chose to go last. The Earth Kings picked Crunch and me to do this event. I'd be the one sending the message. Terrific.

"Think *hard*, big guy," Vince said to Crunch.

"Come on, Jeff, think like an Indian," Dave said. "Use sign language."

Al Nerd handed me a folded sheet of paper. "Don't look at it until you are up in the tree. And, girls, spread out. No talking or planning." He handed Crunch a small pencil and paper to write down the message. "Ready?"

127

Crunch and I shook hands for good luck, then nodded at Al Nerd.

"Ready . . . set . . . Go!"

Crunch took off for the far tree, and I leapt up into the one nearest us. I climbed just about as high as I could, where I'd have a clear view of Crunch in his tree.

I opened the paper and looked at the message I had to send. It said: *SEND HELP*.

How would I ever send this message to Crunch? I looked way over to his tree. He was waving his arms to tell me he was ready. I gave him the OK sign and he began to write that down. I waved my arms to tell him no! no! He understood and crossed out what he had written, then sat there staring at me.

Now what? Then I remembered a game I play at home when my parents have parties. It's called charades. I didn't know if Crunch knew the game or not, so I had to figure he didn't. But still, that kind of sign language ought to work.

Send. How do I do that? What do you send? Mail!

With Crunch watching, I quickly pretended to lick an envelope, seal it, lick a stamp, and then stick it on the envelope. Then I pretended to open a mail box, then put it in. I looked up at Crunch to see if he got the message.

He looked back at me like I was crazy.

I repeated the whole thing.

Crunch rubbed his chin. Then his face brightened. He repeated what I'd done, then nodded to me. I nodded back, and he wrote it down.

Next word: *Help*.

Hmmm. I decided to split this word in half. *hel-p*. *Hel* first. Hmmm. Hell! I put a finger on each side of my head, then I used my arm as a long tail, then I pointed down, way down, and made believe I was hot.

128

Crunch started laughing. I guessed he knew a dirty word when he saw one. He wrote it down, then looked up to me with a questioning look that meant 'But that doesn't make any sense.'

Now, I somehow had to tell him to add a *p* to *hel*. How do you signal *p?*

Then I had it. It was embarrassing, but I had to do it. I crossed my legs, wiggled around, and crossed my legs some more. Everybody on the ground broke up, but my eyes were on Crunch. He was laughing, too, but he was also writing it down! He got it!

Crunch climbed down the tree and sprinted over to Al Nerd and handed him the message. Al Nerd shut off his stopwatch.

"Good job," Al Nerd said. "Let's see if Crunch got the message."

Crunch and I were acting all cocky—until Al Nerd read the message Crunch thought I'd sent.

"Mail a letter to the devil then go to the bathroom."

Crunch was all smiles until he took one look at my face. "That's not it?" Crunch said.

"No," I said. "That's not it."

"Well, what was it?" Crunch asked. "Was I close?"

"Not close at all," I said. "The message was: *Send help.*"

Everybody broke up.

Things didn't look too good for the Earth Kings.

Gwen

CRUNCH and Jeff were like some kind of comedy team on television.

"What!" Crunch said. "*Send help?* That was the message? Why did you do all that stupid stuff with the mail and the devil and having to go to the bathroom?"

Jeff tried to explain it to him, but Crunch just didn't get it.

Now it was our turn. I hoped we wouldn't goof up, too.

Kaybee would be sending the message, and Pinky would be receiving it.

"Good luck," I said. "And think *hard!*"

"Ready . . . set . . . go!"

Pinky sprinted down and shot up her tree. Kaybee was afraid, but soon she climbed hers. She opened her message, thought a minute, then broke three small branches off the tree.

"What's Kaybee doing?" Vince said.

"Beats me," Jeffrey said.

But it wasn't long before we knew exactly what she was doing—and that the Blue Aliens were going to win for sure.

With her three small branches, Kaybee quickly began to form letters. As soon as she formed them, Pinky wrote them down. *C-H-I-E-F-S-I-C-K*. *Chief Sick*. They had it in about one minute.

Pinky jumped out of her tree and was cheering that we won even before she got to Al Nord.

"Way . . . to . . . go!" I yelled. All the Blue Aliens cheered and hugged.

"Girls lead five to four!" Al Nord announced.

"We are in deep trouble," Dave said to the rest of the guys.

"It's Jeff's fault," Crunch said.

"No, it's not!" Jeff yelled.

Vince came between them. "Hey, boys, no good fighting. We've got to stick together. We've got to win the next event or it's all over for the Earth Kings."

"Then let's get 'em!" Crunch said to the guys. "We can do it. Let's do it."

"What's the next event?" Pinky asked.

"The Leaf Hunt," Al Nord said. "You have twenty minutes to find all the different kinds of leaves you can, including evergreen needles. The team with the most leaves, wins."

Jeffrey was bouncing with excitement. And I knew why. I had overheard all the things Dave told Jeff about rocks and trees when we were up on the high ridge.

"Dave, you're our man," Jeffrey said.

"I am, too," Vince said.

"Yeah, but Dave knows leaves," Jeffrey said. "He's studied them. He knows what they look like and he knows where to find them, right, Dave?"

"Bingo," Dave said with a thumbs-up sign.

Tandy and I were to go against them. "Tandy, do you

132

know anything about leaves? Where the different kinds grow and all that?''

Tandy shook her head. "Don't you?"

"Ready . . . set . . . go!"

Dave and Vince ran off into the woods with me and Tandy. Twenty minutes later, we all came back. Dave and Vince returned with so many different kinds of leaves that they had to stuff them inside their shirts just to carry them all. Tandy and I had two handfuls.

"We've got about a hundred different kinds of leaves, everything but the poison ivy leaves," Dave said gleefully. "We left those for the girls."

"Yeah!" Vince said, munching. "And Dave even showed me which leaves you can eat. Mmmm, mint!"

"It's all tied up!" Al Nord announced. "The last event is for the championship!"

Everybody on both sides swallowed loudly.

Al Nord smiled. "Last event is—a compass race!"

"Aren't some of those compasses broken?" Pinky asked.

"I fixed them," Al Nord said. "I replaced the needles. Now, here's how it goes. Everybody is in this race."

"Oh, boy. Great. Cool," we all said.

"Each of you will get a set of compass directions to follow on your own. The first team to have all four of its members reach their destinations is the winner. Ellie and Redwing are out in the woods to keep an eye on you."

Al Nord handed out the compasses. Then he gave each of us a folded piece of paper with the directions.

"Is everybody ready?" Al Nord asked.

We were.

"Ready . . . set . . . go!"

I opened my paper. TWENTY PACES NORTHEAST TO A GREEN ROCK. I started pacing.

133

My directions took me deep into the woods, over the stream twice, around the campfire area, into Redwing's teepee, out of Redwing's teepee, down along the shoreline, over the stream again, back over the stream again, down the dirt road, then right back to the lodge. I was done.

Two other kids were there before me. Kaybee and Dave. They were giggling and laughing like there never was a showdown.

"Did your directions take you back here to the lodge?" I asked.

"Yes," Kaybee said. "Both of us."

I sat down on a wooden porch step to watch the finish.

Pinky came in next. She finished on the other side of the road at the trading post. She came over and sat next to me.

"Looks like we're ahead so far," I said.

"We'll win it" Pinky said.

Then Jeffrey came pacing in. "Nineteen. Twenty!" He sat down beside me. "Three girls, two guys. Terrific."

"Jeffrey, listen," I said. "This paper. I think this is the same kind of paper the thief used."

"I'm not sure, Gwen," he said. "I'll have to compare it to the note the thief left in my pajamas. The note's in my tent."

Then Al Nord appeared in front of us. "I'll take those papers, now."

"We can't keep them?" I asked.

"Nope. I have to check the directions to make sure each of you ended up in the right place."

Al Nord took our compass direction papers.

"There goes your proof," Jeffrey said.

"Not quite," I said with a smile. "I have Kaybee's paper from the tree climb. I can't wait to compare it with your thief note."

134

Then Vince came rolling up. He was concentrating so hard on pacing that he stepped on Jeffrey's toe.

"Yee-ow!" Jeffrey said.

"Oh, sorry," the blimp said. He looked around to see who finished. "Hey, it's a tie so far. Who's out there? Crunch and Tandy, right? If Crunch comes in first, we win! Come on Crunch!"

"Come on, Tandy!" Pinky yelled.

Everybody got up to watch the big finish. We stared between the trees around us to see who would appear first.

The bushes over to our left started shaking around.

"Someone's coming!" I shouted.

The branches parted.

A foot appeared.

"It's Crunch!" Vince screamed. "We won!"

Crunch was still about thirty yards away. He looked up when Vince yelled, and Crunch came running right for us.

"Earth Kings! Earth Kings!" Crunch yelled.

Al Nord came up and took Crunch's paper, along with Pinky's and Vince's.

Suddenly we heard a voice behind us.

"Watch out!" It was Tandy. Her head was down, and she was counting her paces. "Eighteen. Nineteen. Twenty!" Her last pace put her face-to-face with Crunch.

Crunch smiled. "Too late. We already won."

"Awwwwww!" Tandy groaned.

Vince screamed, "The Earth Kings are champions of the world!"

"Not quite," Al Nord said.

"Huh?" Vince said.

Everybody fell silent.

"All the directions led right here to the lodge," Al Nord said, "except two."

"That's right," Pinky said. "My directions ended at the trading post. Who's the second person?"

Al Nord turned to his left. "Crunch is. Sorry, Crunch, you goofed your last direction."

"But, but, but," Crunch said.

"You ran over here where the rest of the kids were, instead of pacing off your true direction to the trading post."

"But, but, but."

"So," Al Nord said, "you are disqualified. Girls, you are the champions!"

"YAAAAAAAAAAAAAAAAAY!"

After we got hoarse from screaming "Blue Aliens! Blue Aliens!" a million times, we remembered what Al Nord had said earlier.

"Oh, boy!" Pinky said. "We get to throw Al and Redwing in the lake!"

Redwing, who was watching all this from the porch, said, "Um, I think I hear the Spirit of the Forest calling me."

"Oh, no!" Tandy said.

"Come on, guys," I called to the boys, "we can't do this alone. Crunch, grab Al's leg. Vince, grab his other leg. Dave and Jeff, go round up Redwing!"

"Let's get 'em, Earth Kings!" fat Vince shouted.

We picked up the two counselors and carried them through the lodge toward the lake. Ellie Nord was sitting in a chair reading a book as we marched through.

"So, they got you, huh?" she said, laughing at her husband. "Have a nice dip, honey!"

Vince looked at me. I looked at Crunch. Crunch looked at Pinky. Pinky looked at Jeff who looked at Tandy who looked back to Vince who looked at Crunch.

"Let's get her!" Vince roared.

"No!" Ellie shrieked. She jumped up and tried to hide behind her chair, but soon we had her right beside Al Nord. We all went outside toward the lake.

"Charge!" Crunch screamed.

All of us got behind the three victims, and pushed and ran them right into the water. The only trouble was, we went in with them.

Fifteen minutes later, we all sat sopping wet on the back porch of the lodge.

"You kids are creeps!" Ellie said, trying to comb some stringy brown stuff out of her blond hair.

"Blue Aliens are the best!" Pinky yelled. "Hey, guys, how's it feel to be losers, huh?"

"Aw, you girls won by dumb luck," Vince said.

"Dumb?" Kaybee said.

"Yeah," Jeff said. "If we had any competitions with real brain work, we'd smear you."

"Sure you would," I giggled.

"You just name it," Pinky said. "Go on, big mouth, challenge us. I dare you."

"Okay, Pinky," Jeffrey said. "You think you're so smart, how come you couldn't figure out who the sneak thief is?"

"She did figure it out," Crunch said. "She figured it out a long time ago, because *she's* the thief!"

"I am not!" Pinky said.

"Then prove it!" Vince said.

"Afraid, Pinky?" Jeffrey said. "Afraid we'll find out it's you?"

"Okay, you're on!" Pinky said, just about burning up. "Our brains against your pumpkin heads. We're already champions of the camp, so it will be no problem beating losers like you."

"Well, well," Al Nord said, "this should be good. A

137

contest to play detectives and find the sneak thief. I like it. You have a little over an hour till the campfire cookout dinner. Better get going.''

The boys rushed off to start thinking and investigating.

"Pinky," I said, "how are we going to find out who the thief is?"

"Beats me," Pinky said. "But the boys won't find out either. They'll just make fools of themselves."

"Unless they really do find out."

"Ha! They'll never do it." Pinky walked off.

Why was Pinky so sure the boys wouldn't uncover the thief? I wondered. Was Crunch right—could she be the one? There was one way to find out—the notepaper from the tree climb. Somehow I had to compare it to the thief's note Jeffrey had. If they were the same, Al Nord was probably the thief because the paper was from his office. I was absolutely certain I was right. Well, almost certain.

Jeff

GWEN came over to try and trick me into showing her the thief's note I'd saved. I told her, gee, I was sorry, but I couldn't find it.

It was in my back pocket the whole time. I just couldn't take the risk that Gwen's theory was right. I had to try out my own theory first.

Now we were all out in the woods by the campfire. The sun was about six inches from setting.

"So, Jeff," Pinky said, "has your great brain solved anything?"

"Maybe," I said, "and maybe not. Has yours?"

Crunch said, "Jeff, you know Pinky can't find the thief until she finds her brain first."

I burst out laughing and turned toward the fire.

"Hey, Jeff," Pinky said. "Don't melt your sneakers again. Why don't you turn around and melt your face this time?"

"It wouldn't help," I said, "you'd still win the Miss Ugly Contest."

I grinned at her.

She stuck out her tongue.

Otto and Happy were cooking chicken over the fire and it smelled great.

Dave and Kaybee were sitting together. They kept pushing a twig around the ground between them. Maybe Kaybee was explaining the movement of the universe. Maybe Dave was just playing racing cars. Who knows?

"Pinky," Tandy said, stretching out on her back and looking up at the orange sky, "what's the thing you want most in the world?"

"Money," Pinky said. "And fame. And beauty. And straight A's, and new clothes, and good-looking guys, and. . ."

We all laughed. Then Gwen said, "So, Tandy, what do you really want, most in the whole world?"

"Right now?" Tandy said. "Right now I wouldn't mind having this weekend to do all over again."

Wow, I thought. It was amazing. Tandy sure had changed since she'd been here. In about two days, she'd gone from a whining wimp to a girl who discovered that winning is a whole lot better than whining. Heck, I thought, even *losing* is a whole lot better than whining.

"Know what I want, Jeffrey?" Gwen asked. "I can't *wait* to see your brilliant solution to the sneak thief mystery. How about it?"

I just grinned at her. Me and my big mouth.

Al Nerd must have overheard Gwen. He turned from chatting with Ellie and Redwing and said, "So what about it, kids? Who's the villain? Who took Gwen's book, and Jeff's pajamas, and Tandy's bear, and Crunch's comic, and Vince's candy, and my whistle?"

We all looked at each other. We knew one of us was the thief, but no had discovered who. It was weird.

"I don't have an answer yet," Vince said, "but Crunch

and I were talking the whole thing over. Only three kids weren't hit by the thief. Kaybee, Pinky, and Dave. Maybe it's one of them."

Tandy spoke up. "Redwing and Ellie Nord didn't have anything stolen either. Neither did Otto or Happy."

Otto and Happy lifted their heads from their cooking and looked surprised.

"Don't get them mad," Dave whispered to Tandy. "They might feed us roast groundhog or something."

"There are a lot of reasons why some people might not have had things stolen," Al Nerd said. "Remember, the thief might have even stolen from himself or herself so he or she wouldn't be suspected."

"I think it's Pinky," Vince said. "She was the one behind all the dirty tricks. I never trusted her. I'll bet she's the thief."

"Ridiculous," Pinky said. "Maybe it's you, fatso."

"Sure," Vince said. "I always hide my candy in a cave."

"Zounders!" Kaybee said. "A zooming thought just hit my mind. What if there is more than one thief? Or, what if everybody stole something as a trick?"

We all thought about that. It was possible, I guessed. After someone pulled the first theft of Gwen's book, the next thief just imitated what the first thief had done. Possible. But I didn't think so.

"Well, bean brain?" Pinky said to me.

"Okay," I said. "I have a surefire way to catch the thief."

Everybody stopped what they were doing and looked up at me. Even Otto and Happy stopped turning the chickens.

"Well, Jeff," Al Nerd said, "go to it."

I reached in my pocket and took out an arrowhead and held it up so everyone could see it. "Exhibit A. I found this arrowhead a few feet from where Crunch's stolen comic book was discovered. I figure the thief dropped it. I figure whoever doesn't have an arrowhead is the thief. I asked you before and got nowhere. Now, I'm asking you again. Lemme see your arrowheads."

"Mine's at my tent," Tandy said. "Be right back." She ran off.

I looked down at Gwen. She held up her arrowhead so everybody could see.

I looked at Vince. He held his up.

Crunch waved his arrowhead in the air.

Kaybee held hers up, upside down.

Pinky showed me her arrowhead.

Dave was struggling around inside his pockets. "It's here somewhere, I know it is."

I waited, getting kind of sweaty. Was the thief Dave?

"What's taking Tandy so long?" Vince asked.

"There!" Dave held up his arrowhead.

I smiled. "Well, folks, we've caught our thief. And it's Tandy. She's the only one who doesn't have an arrowhead, and it looks to me like she's run away."

"I don't believe it!" Pinky said.

"Facts don't lie," I said, bouncing on my toes.

Just then we heard running footsteps. Tandy ran into the circle of kids.

"Whew!" she said. "I couldn't find it. Forgot where I put it. Here it is!"

Tandy held up her arrowhead for everyone to see.

"I don't get it," I said.

Pinky suddenly stood up. "Wait a minute," she said. "Jeff, where's your arrowhead?"

"It's right here," I said, holding it up.

"No," Pinky said. "That's the arrowhead you said you

found. If that's true, you should have *two* arrowheads. So, where's yours?''

Uh-oh.

"You just made up the whole thing!" Pinky said. "You thought you'd fool somebody into confessing! What a dummy!"

"Hold it, hold it, hold it," I said. "I did find this arrowhead, I swear. And I did have two, honest."

"Yeah, sure," Pinky said.

"Listen," I said, "Redwing handed out eight arrowheads. And here they all are. I'm not lying about finding one. Gwen was with me when I found it. So, the thief ripped off mine!"

"Nice try, J.M.," Gwen said. "But the thief outwitted you. I wish you hadn't lost that thief's note."

"Yeah," I said. I had to think. I knew I was close to an answer, I just knew it. Think, brain, think!

"Dinnertime's here!" Otto said.

We each got a lap tray and lined up for Otto's and Happy's chicken, corn on the cob, and baked potatoes cooked over an open fire. Naturally, there was plenty of dragonfly blood.

"This is great!" Crunch said.

"Sure is," Vince said, craning his neck toward the fire. "And there's plenty more, too!"

"You know, Jeff," Gwen said, chewing, "one thing bothers me. How did the thief sneak in and out of everyone's tent so quickly? It seems to me that only somebody really familiar with where we all put stuff could do that. Maybe Kaybee's right, maybe each of us is sharing a tent with a thief."

At first, I thought that idea was stupid. Then I got to thinking about it. Something Gwen had just said made sense.

Then, halfway through my fourth bite of chicken, my brain suddenly shifted all the pieces of the puzzle together. Why hadn't I thought of it before?

"I've got it!" I yelled.

"Again?" Pinky said.

"My pajamas were stolen, right?" I said.

"Yes, Dumbo, they were," Crunch said.

"And they were stolen out of my suitcase," I said.

"That means whoever stole them had to know I had those pajamas."

"So?" Tandy said.

"So, only one person in the whole camp knew I had Dumbo pajamas."

"Who?" Crunch asked.

Vince slapped his forehead. "Who else, dummy. It's the kid Jeff's been sharing a tent with. It's *Dave!*"

"Dave!" Kaybee shrieked.

All eyes locked on Dave's freckled face.

"Whoa," Dave said. "Me? You have to be kidding. Me? I've got to write this down, Jeffrey, and send it in to the newspapers or *Ripley's Believe It Or Not.*"

Dave took a pencil and a piece of paper from his back pocket. "Now, how did that go again? I wore your pajamas while I stole your arrowhead . . ."

All the other kids were laughing at Dave's antics.

My eyes were so wide with excitement they were burning.

I walked over to Dave. I took the piece of paper out of his hand. I held up the piece of paper so everybody could see it.

"Dave's paper," I said.

I reached into my back pocket and took out the note the thief had left on my pajamas.

"The thief's note," I said.

"Hey!" Gwen said, "I thought you lost that."

I grinned at her and shrugged.

"The papers match!" Pinky said.

Al Nerd was on his feet. He came over and took the two pieces of paper and held them up in the light of the campfire. "They're identical. Same watermarks. And they came from my office. You even took my paper, too?" he said to Dave.

"Heh-heh," Dave said. He reached into his pocket and took out an arrowhead. He held it out to me. "I believe this is yours, Jeff. I'll trade you for mine."

"He *is* the thief!" Pinky said.

"David?" Kaybee said. "Are you this thieving person?"

"Thieving?" Dave said. "I wouldn't call it thieving. Practical jokes, maybe, but not thieving."

"He *did* do it!" Tandy said, moving away from him.

"Yaaay!" Vince said. "Jeff caught the thief! The Earth Kings win the investigation!"

Crunch turned to Vince. "Who cares? Calm down, Turtle, I wanna hear what Dave has to say."

"So do I!" Al Nerd said.

"Spill it, creep," Pinky said.

"I'll talk, I'll talk, coppers!" Dave said, laughing. "It was a gag, what can I say? When I pulled the first gag on Gwen, I had so much fun I just had to do it to somebody else. I didn't know the whole thing would turn into a worldwide manhunt."

"Why?" Al Nerd said. "Why'd you do it?"

"You want the truth?" Dave said. "Okay, I'll tell you." Dave got serious and he looked each of us in the eye. "Because you guys made me sick. You really did. We came here to have fun, and you guys did nothing but get mad and fight. Me, I wanted to have fun, but I couldn't because of all of you. So, instead of getting mad and all fired-up like you creeps, I decided to have some fun of my own. But now I'm sorry. I really am. How did I know we'd all end up getting along?''

Nobody said anything for a minute. We knew exactly how he felt.

"I say it makes sense," I said. "Dave's my buddy and I know what he means. He was just trying to have fun—like we were all *supposed* to be doing. And even though he stuck my Dumbo pajamas up for everybody to see, I forgive him. But I sure would like to get back at him.''

Dave laughed a little.

"I agreed," Gwen said. "He stole my book, but he made sure I got it back, didn't he? We all got our things back.''

"And," Kaybee said, "who knows?''

"Who knows what?'' Tandy said.

"Who knows," Kaybee said, "if it weren't for David's pranksterish pranks, we might still be fighting a war in the woods.''

"Hold it," Pinky said. "Nobody is going to convince me that what Dave did was good.''

"What are you complaining about?'' Crunch said. "He didn't take anything of yours and make you feel like a fool in front of everybody.''

"Yeah," Pinky said to Dave, "why didn't you take anything of mine?''

Dave shrugged. "After you caught us trying to put a frog in your bed, I figured you'd kill me if I did any more.''

"She would have!'' Vince said. "That girl is a toughie!''

"What about Kaybee?'' Tandy asked. "How come you didn't steal from her and embarrass her?''

Dave shrugged and said nothing.

"He likes her, that's why!'' Pinky said.

"Awwww,'' Crunch said.

Dave turned beet red.

"Let's take a vote," I said. "All in favor of forgiving Dave for his horrible, stinky, sneaky, and pretty funny gags, raise your hand."

Everybody raised a hand—except Crunch. We all looked at him.

"We forgot one thing," Crunch said. "Mack. Mack said he saw a ghost. Dave, did you do that?"

"No," Dave said. "Honest. I'd never be mean enough to scare anybody like that."

"So, who did it?" Tandy asked.

"Awww, Mack scared himself," Vince said.

"I don't think so," Al Nerd said. "Mack told me he actually saw something, and I think he did."

All our heads turned toward Redwing.

"Hey, not me!" Redwing said. "The Spirit of the Forest had the night off."

"Then who did it?" I said.

Nobody moved.

Then, Gwen raised her hand. "I did it."

"WHAT?"

"I did it, I did it," Gwen said. "Sorry, but I did it. Dave was right about our fighting in the beginning. It really brought the worst out in all of us. I'll tell the truth. Vince, I like you now, I really do. But in the beginning, all the boys were really mean to us girls, but you were the worst. You rubbed it in over the volleyball game, the frog races, and everything. And after all our clothes were tied together, you made even more fun of us for being scared. So, I decided to get back at you and scare you. I put a sheet over my head and drew a horrible face on it with a marking pen. Then I headed over to your tent. But Mack was going there too, because he'd had a fight with Crunch.

147

I saw Mack and he saw me. He screamed bloody murder and I took off. I feel awful about it. Poor Mack.''

"What'd he do when he saw you?'' Tandy asked.

"First he stopped dead in his tracks,'' Gwen said. "Then his mouth just kind of dropped open.''

Vince covered a giggle with his hand.

"Then his eyes flew wide and he sucked in his breath like this: *Huuuuuuk!*''

"*Pfft!*'' Pinky let a burst of laughter escape.

"Then,'' Gwen continued, starting to smile, "he dropped his pillow and blanket, stepped back and . . . fell on his butt.'' She started to laugh. "It's not funny!''

Oh, but it was. It was the funniest thing I'd ever heard. Laughter spread like wildfire around the campfire until everybody, including Gwen, was laughing like monkeys.

Soon we all settled down, ate some more, sang some songs, then wandered back to our tents to pack up our things. Our parents would be picking us up in about a half an hour.

148

Gwen

ALL the girls said our good-byes up in my tent.

"Pinky," I said, "How about we call a truce. Peace?"

"Sure, why not," Pinky said.

We shook hands, and she squeezed. So I squeezed harder.

"This was the best weekend of my life," Tandy announced. "I learned not to be a wimp."

"So why are you still hugging your wimpy teddy bear?" Pinky said.

Tandy smiled. "For the same reason you had to have that battery-powered Flintstones night-light on when you went to sleep."

"I told you never to tell anybody!" Pinky shouted.

"And I told you never to call me a wimp!"

Pinky thought about that. "Okay, it's a deal."

Pinky and Tandy shook hands. Then Tandy couldn't help herself: she hugged Pinky.

Pinky said, "And if you ever tell anyone what Tandy just said, Gwen . . ."

"Don't worry," I said, "your silly secret is safe with me."

"With me, too," Kaybee said. "But I've never been scared by the nighttime. It's the daytime that scares me!"

"You are really wild," Tandy said. "But I like you. See you in September, Kaybee."

"And I'll see you in there, too," Kaybee said, moving immediately to give Tandy a huge hug. Then she tried to hug Pinky, who ducked, so Kaybee hugged me instead.

At ten minutes of nine, all of us gathered in the main lodge with all our suitcases. The guys were shaking hands and trying to act like grown-up men as they said good-bye.

"Hang in there, buddy," Vince said to Jeff, shaking his hand.

"You got it," Jeffrey said gruffly. "Crunch, hang tough."

"Bingo," Crunch said, shaking Jeff's hand. "Have an explosive summer, got me?"

"Got you."

"Dave?" Vince said. "Keep rolling, hotshot."

"You keep rolling, too," Dave said. "Whoops, sorry—that really wasn't a fat joke."

"Forget it," Vince said. "Doesn't bother a big boy like me. The bigger they are, the better they are. That's my motto."

"You got it," Dave said.

Guys, geesh.

"Well, guys," I said. "I had fun. Guess we'll see you in school."

The guys were too embarrassed to get too friendly. They stayed in their little group, smiled, mumbled, and kind of nodded at us girls.

"Well," Al Nord said, "it has been quite an interesting weekend, kids."

"It certainly has," Ellie Nord said. "I almost wish I was a kid again so *I* could steal your whistle!"

150

"And I, for one, am glad that the trouble is over," Redwing said. "There's a ball game I want to watch in my teepee tonight! Really, I had a good time."

"Me, too," Jeffrey said. He walked up and shook Al Nord's hand. "You might lecture too much, but your games were first-class. We've decided to make you an official Earth King."

For a second there, I was sure Al Nord was going to cry. But he fought back the tears and just laughed and flexed his muscles and said so long to the boys.

"And you, too, Redwing," Vince said. "Come on, join the Earth Kings!"

"Yeah," Dave said, "you've got good team *spirit!*"

The girls and I walked over to Ellie Nord and thanked her for being so nice and for what she did for poor Carmen. We hugged and didn't do any of the stupid stuff like the guys.

"Almost forgot!" Jeff said. "Hey, Dave, you left something behind in the tent."

"I did?" Dave said.

"Yeah," Jeffrey said. Out of his backpack he pulled a doll. "Yeah, Dave, you forgot your Talky Taffy doll."

"Hey! You—you stole it! I—you—" Dave didn't know what to say.

We couldn't believe it! We all started laughing like crazy.

"Davie has a dolly?" Crunch roared.

"It's not mine!" Dave said. "My—my sister stuck it into my bag at the last minute as a joke. It's hers, honest!"

"Suuurrre it is!" Pinky said. "Awww, it's so cute."

"Make it talk, Dave, make it talk!" Vince said.

Dave snatched the Talky Taffy doll out of Jeff's hand and shoved it headfirst into his bag. It said: *"Mommeeeeeee."*

We all broke up.

Jeff was beaming. He was so proud of himself for finally getting back at Dave. We were all proud of him because he got back at Dave for all of us.

A minute later, we heard the crunching of tires outside the lodge. A long silver Cadillac was idling out front.

"My parents," Tandy said. "Well, I guess I'll see all you guys later."

"Bye, Tandy," we said.

When Tandy got outside, her mother was waiting beside the car with open arms.

"Here she is, my little girl!" her mother cooed. "We missed you *sooo* much. We were worrying about you the *whole* time. Was it so horrible, honey? Did you have at least a *little* fun, my darling?"

Tandy stopped and looked up at her mother. "Oh, Mom, don't be such a wimp."

She walked briskly past her wide-eyed mom, and just before Tandy stepped inside the Cadillac she turned back and gave us a big wink.

"Well, J.M.," I said, "you did it, you cracked the mystery of the creepy camp thief."

"Yeah, and you girls won the camp championship," he said.

"So, what are you going to do for the rest of the summer?" I asked.

Jeffrey shrugged. "Beats me. Maybe I'll treat you to lunch at Big Burger a few times."

"Really?"

"Yeah, my aim with that french fry was just a little bit off, and I could use the practice!"

I thwacked him on the arm, and we both had a good laugh.